HAUNTED

THE RIVERBOAT PHANTOM

CHRIS EBOCH

ALADDIN
NEW YORK LONDON TORONTO SYDNEY

ALADDIN

An imprint of Simon & Schuster Children's Publishing Division

1230 Avenue of the Americas, New York, NY 10020

First Aladdin paperback edition August 2009

Text copyright © 2009 by Chris Eboch

All rights reserved, including the right of reproduction in whole or in part in any form.

ALADDIN is a trademark of Simon & Schuster, Inc., and related logo is a registered trademark of Simon & Schuster, Inc.

For information about special discounts for bulk purchases, please contact Simon & Schuster Special Sales at 1-866-506-1949 or business@simonandschuster.com.

The Simon & Schuster Speakers Bureau can bring authors to your live event. For more information or to book an event contact the Simon & Schuster Speakers Bureau at 1-866-248-3049 or visit our website at www.simonspeakers.com.

Designed by Lisa Vega

The text of this book was set in Minister Std.

Manufactured in the United States of America

10 9 8 7 6 5 4 3 2 1

Library of Congress Control Number 2008942155

ISBN 978-1-4169-7549-6

ISBN 978-1-4169-9628-6 (eBook)

For Lucy Hampson, with love

ACKNOWLEDGMENTS

Many people helped with the research and fact-checking for this book. Alan L. Bates gave detailed feedback on steamboat workings and terminology. Dale Flick suggested resources. The members of the Northwest Steam Society arranged a visit to a working steamboat, the *Virginia V*, a beautiful Mosquito Fleet steamer in Seattle. NSS Treasurer Stephanie Hylton and Secretary and *Steam Gage* publisher Jenni Kane reviewed the manuscript.

I also greatly appreciate the hospitality and information provided by the crew of the *Virginia V*, especially Senior Captain Dale Pederson and Assistant Captain Eric Reinholdtsen, who made me feel welcome, and Fireman Gary Frankel, who explained everything about the boiler room.

For more information on steamboats, visit SteamBoats.com, SteamBoats.org, or VirginiaV.org.

HAUNTED

THE RIVERBOAT PHANTOM

CHAPTER

1

can't wait to meet this ghost!"

"Shh!" I hissed. "Lower your voice. Or at least don't talk like you expect to see the ghost yourself. You could say something like, 'I can't wait to learn about the ghost.' Then it wouldn't matter if people overhear."

Tania nodded absently, her eyes on the steamboat ahead. I followed her gaze. I was psyched about the trip. I'd never been on a steamboat, and this one was a beauty, old-fashioned and fancy. It had a real paddle wheel! On the top deck, a flag whipped in the wind. The air smelled of river water, and gasoline from the boat.

We were on a dock in a small town on the Mississippi River, somewhere north of Saint Louis. We'd head down the river, just Mom, my sister, and me—and the crew of the *Haunted* TV show. The fact that we were investigating a ghost story, and my sister could really see ghosts, made it just that much better. Even if I couldn't see ghosts myself, I could expect an adventure.

"I can see why they wanted to investigate this ghost," I said. "A steamship pilot who crashed the boat. Pretty dramatic." I leaned closer and whispered, "See any sign of him?"

"Not yet." Tania glanced around, and then wrinkled her nose. "This would be great, if it weren't for *her*," she muttered.

I didn't have to follow my sister's gaze to know whom she meant. Madame Natasha stood on the dock a few yards from us. Her gauzy blue-and-green dress fluttered in the wind, her red hair topping it like a candle flame. She had her eyes closed, and her face was pinched in this expression that was probably supposed to be spiritual. She'd said she wanted to start "tuning in to the vibrations," if you can believe that.

I found Madame Natasha annoying, but it was even worse for Tania. She could see ghosts, but didn't want anyone to know about it. The fake psychic said she saw ghosts, and wanted everyone to know about it. Tania knew Madame Natasha was only pretending, and the stories she made up were all wrong.

I watched the TV crew board the boat. Most of them I recognized from the first time we traveled with them, a month ago, though I didn't know them well. My heart jumped when I spotted Maggie, the production assistant. She grinned and waved. I felt my face go red as I waved back.

Mom hurried around the deck, checking on everyone. She saw me watching and called out, "Not long now!"

Right. I'd learned something about TV shows. When you see them on TV, they're usually exciting, because something is happening all the time. But when they're shooting a TV show, mostly nothing is happening. It's just people moving around, setting up equipment, calling out commands, and complaining that things aren't working right. It takes forever.

"Let's get on now," I said, "before they start shooting. We can explore the ship."

Tania's gaze flicked between the ship and Madame Natasha. "I don't know. I want to see that fraud's first encounter. I want to hear what lies she makes up."

I glanced over at Madame Natasha. She was standing in full sun, probably to make her colors brighter. But I guess she hadn't yet learned the lesson about slow TV shows. Sweat beaded on her forehead, and her hair looked limp. The makeup artist came down to dab more powder on her face, as if she didn't already have enough.

"We'll have a better view from on the ship," I said.

Tania shrugged and nodded. "I guess we'd better

get behind the cameras before they start filming."

We went up the gangplank, dodging TV show staff and the boat's crew. The sailors were all in old-fashioned clothes. The ship usually did river cruises, and I guess the old costumes were part of the deal.

We checked out the main deck, then took steep stairs up to the second level. If we leaned over the railing, we had a good view of the gangplank and the open part of the lower deck. Bruce, my stepfather and producer of *Haunted*, stood in front of the camera and beamed. Someone called out, "Action!"

"Welcome to *Haunted*, where we delve into the questions of the spirit world. We're here today on the *Delta Belle* steamboat, one of the rare survivors from the great era of steamboat river traffic. This beautiful ship was built in 1920. A mere six years later, the ship hit a snag in the river, a buried tree that tore through its hull. Many passengers and crew died that day—and it is said that one of them still haunts the ship! We're here to see if we can reach that ghost. To start, we have our special guest, the psychic Madame Natasha. Let's watch her first entrance to the ship. Will she pick up on vibrations from the spirit world?"

Tania leaned close to me and whispered, "I can't wait to see this."

"Speaking of seeing things, do you see anyone else? I mean, anyone I can't see?"

Tania shaded her eyes and scanned the deck. "No. No ghosts here. So if that fraud says she sees one, she's lying."

I considered this. "That's assuming you still see every ghost there is. We don't know that for sure."

Tania looked up with wide eyes. "But I have to!"

My sister's on a mission to save all ghosts. "Remember what you read? Sometimes preteen girls see ghosts, but then stop seeing them as they grow up."

"But I'm not a teenager yet! I'm only eleven."

"Yes, but we can't assume it will stop exactly on your thirteenth birthday. We don't know for sure. I'm just saying you should be prepared for disappointment."

Tania slumped down and scowled. Personally, I wouldn't mind so much if she never saw another ghost. The last one almost killed her. Sure, Tania will insist it wasn't the ghost's fault. She didn't mean any harm. But what difference does that make, when you're possessed by a crazy ghost that makes you ice-cold? And I was the one who had to protect Tania, help her help the ghost, and keep it all a secret from our parents and the TV crew.

I didn't even get to see the ghost. I guess I'm not "sensitive" enough. Doesn't life stink sometimes?

Madame Natasha slowly came up the gangplank. I think she was trying to look floaty, but it ruined the effect when she tripped at the top. She recovered and took a few steps onto the deck. She closed her eyes, held up her hands, and tossed her head back and forth a few times. "The spirit vibrations are so strong! So much pain. Oh!"

She dropped her hands and staggered back a step. I was hoping she'd step onto the gangplank and fall down it, but no such luck.

She had her head bowed, and I think she was moaning, though I couldn't quite hear. Then her head snapped up and her eyes opened, staring straight ahead. She reached out a hand as if offering to shake. "Yes. Yes, I can hear you. We're here to help you move on to a better place. I will help you pass through the veil, so you may rest in peace."

From behind the camera, Bruce started waving his hands and mouthing something. Madame Natasha glanced at him and added, "After we hear your story." Bruce nodded.

Tania turned away with a sound of disgust. "That's the most ridiculous thing I've ever seen. Come on, I want to find the real ghost."

We went all over the ship. The bottom deck was

the largest, with about twenty feet of open space at the front of the boat. That was where they'd filmed Madame Natasha. The boiler room was toward the front, and the engine room at the back. Staterooms surrounded them. The paddle wheel, at the back of the boat, rose as high as the third deck.

Stairs led up to the next level. A sign said it was called the boiler deck, even though the boiler was below. A walkway went around the deck, with railings on the outside. That level had an enormous lounge, a kitchen, and a big dining room where waiters were setting the tables.

We went on up to the third level, which was called the hurricane deck for some reason. It had the same kind of open passage all the way around, with railings to keep people from falling off. I don't think I'd want to be up there in a hurricane, though. This level held more staterooms.

Finally, the top deck was open except for a tiny pilothouse and black smokestacks rising into the air. The sign said the deck was called the Texas roof. Where did they get these names?

The pilothouse had windows in a curve around the front and sides. We peered through a side window. Four men stood inside, dressed fancy in buttoned-up vests and hats and things. A big guy with a mustache had one hand on the enormous wheel. He glanced at us, grinned, and lifted the other hand to pull a cord.

Whoo-whoooot!

The sound of the whistle made my heart leap in a funny way, and I found myself grinning back. Steam billowed out of the smokestack just behind the pilothouse. The captain's hand dropped to the wheel, and we were moving.

I swung around to look over the front of the boat as we pulled away from the dock and out into the river.

"All gone, sir!" one of the men called.

"Maybe they'll let us go in and watch him steer," I said.

Tania didn't glance at me. "But where's the ghost! I want to find him."

I sighed. "Can't you just relax and have fun?"

She turned her big blue eyes on me and just *looked*. I sighed again. No, she couldn't just have fun. "Well, where else do you want to look, then?" I grumbled. I wondered again—what if there was no ghost? The last time, I had trouble even believing Tania. I thought she might be crazy, or lying, or . . . *something*. Ghosts couldn't be real. Even after seeing one possess her, I hadn't seen the ghost itself. The more time passed, the more my skepticism was coming back. And even if some ghosts were real, who was to say this one was?

"What about down below?" she said. "In the . . . the hold, or whatever? There must be a lower deck."

I shrugged. "Let's look."

We went to the first deck again. As we poked around, I had the strangest feeling. Like someone was watching me.

CHAPTER

I glanced over my shoulder. Nothing. I tried to shake off the feeling.

A moment later, I was looking back again. The passageway was clear, but a shadow stretched out from the corner we'd just turned. Well, why not a shadow? It was a sunny morning, and people—living people—threw shadows. But we'd just come around that corner, and no one else had been there.

Tania had gone on. I grunted and followed her. I wasn't here to worry about shadows.

I wouldn't let myself look back as I went along the passage. Not until I got to the end. As I turned the corner, I couldn't help but glance over my shoulder.

A dark shape disappeared into a side passage. I'd only had a glimpse, but it didn't quite look human. The outline was too blurry, and transparent at the edges.

The hair prickled on the back of my neck. Was it the

ghost? I wasn't supposed to be able to see ghosts—was I? All this ghost stuff was still new, and we didn't really know the rules.

I wasn't sure if I should tell Tania. She'd go charging after the whatever. But what if it was nothing—my imagination, or one of the crew who just happened to be nearby? Or some person spying on us. That was a creepy thought, but I didn't know why anyone would bother.

Or maybe it was the ghost. Maybe I'd actually seen it myself! So why was it acting so strange? The last ghost didn't sneak around. She just hung around the stairs where she died. She'd been happy to find out that Tania could see her—well, as happy as a wailing, insane ghost ever gets.

So I kept my mouth shut, and just kept glancing over my shoulder until my neck hurt. We couldn't find any way farther down, unless it was from inside the boiler room. We hesitated outside the door and exchanged glances. A boiler room didn't sound like the kind of place tourists were invited to visit.

A man came out of the room. He was dressed in a different kind of old-fashioned outfit from the men in the pilothouse—rough shirt, suspenders holding up dark pants, and a soft cap.

"Excuse me," Tania said, "can you tell us how to get down below?"

He grinned. "Ain't no down below. This is a river-boat!"

Tania frowned. "And what is that supposed to mean?" She doesn't like it when people sound condescending—who does?

"It means she only draws three feet of water."

Tania and I looked at each other blankly. The man grinned even wider, and went on. "This here river is shallow—only five or six feet in places. Takes a shallow boat to get through. Riverboats have flat bottoms, everything carried above the water. They can slide right over sandbars and snags. A riverboat's just an engine on a raft." He grinned and winked. "They say the best riverboats can travel straight across a meadow, so long as there's dew on the grass."

"Oh." Tania bit her lip. "So there's nothing below? This is it?"

"That's right, honey."

I pointed to the boiler room. "Can we look in there?" I really just wanted to see it for myself, but Tania shot me a grateful look.

"Sure, take a peek." He opened the door and let us look through. His Old South accent slipped a bit as he said, "This isn't quite how it was in the old days. They've made it a lot safer. Boilers used to blow up all the time." Tania's eyes widened, and he gave her a wink.

The accent came back. "Don't you worry, honey, we's as safe as your room at home nowadays."

We looked around at all the machinery and pipes. Everything looked clean and freshly painted, not that old. The air hummed with a sound like a powerful fan. I wished I could take a closer look at it all, but they were busy working.

"It's a great ship," I said.

"Don't say that!" He looked outraged. Then he grinned. "Ships sail on the seas. On the river, it's a boat."

"Right. Okay, thanks."

He went inside and closed the door. "So no ghost?" I said.

Tania's eyes widened as she looked past me. "No, not a ghost of a chance that I'm going in there!" She laughed brightly. Before I could ask her what the heck she meant, she said, "Hi, Mom!"

Oh. This ghost-tracking thing would be easier if we weren't trying to keep it a secret from everyone else who thinks *they're* the ghost hunters.

"Isn't this a beautiful ship!" Mom exclaimed.

"Boat, Mom," I said. "On the river, we call them boats."

Mom messed with my hair. "Maggie tells me they used to call them floating palaces."

Maggie joined us and smiled. My heart gave a bump. "Fancy riverboats, like this," she said. "Lots of boats just carried cargo and kept it simple, but passenger boats pulled out the works. Have you seen the dining room? Dinner is in a few minutes."

She led us to it. We'd just glanced in before, only interested in finding a ghost. Now I saw what she meant. Mirrors in gilt frames lined the walls and made the room look bigger. Crystal chandeliers hung from the ceiling. Every piece of ceiling and wall had fancy carved wood-work. The chairs were big and plush, the tables covered with white tablecloths, china, and glassware.

"We're at Captain Dale's table," Mom said as proud as if she were an honored guest, and not just in charge of the show that was paying for this trip.

We settled ourselves. I had Tania on one side of me, and Maggie on the other. I couldn't think of anything to say, so I looked at the paper menu set on my plate. It listed what we would get for soup, salad, main course, and dessert. It was a good thing we didn't have choices, because I couldn't understand a single thing listed. I think it was French. The silverware was heavy, and of some different metal than ours at home. Maybe real silver. All this might have been pretty, but I didn't like it. I had three forks and two spoons. How was I supposed to know which to use?

In a few minutes, the captain joined us. He was the big man from the pilothouse. He wore a black jacket over a buttoned-up white vest, with an actual pocket watch on a chain. His mustache was long and droopy— old-fashioned like the rest of him.

He greeted us with a friendly smile, and waiters brought our salads. I reached for a fork and hesitated. I tried to see which one other people were using. Maggie leaned over, so close I could feel her breath on my cheek. "Start from the outside and work your way in." She touched her own silverware. "Salad fork, dinner fork. The little one on top's for dessert. Big spoon for soup, little one for coffee."

I gave her a smile, half grateful, half embarrassed, and dug into my food. The grown-ups chatted. Madame Natasha sat across from Tania and talked loudly about emanations and manifestations and stuff. Bruce, next to her, hung on every word. I caught Mom giving them a few dirty looks.

Tania fidgeted more than usual. She kept putting down her fork, craning her neck to look around, and then sinking down into her chair with a sigh.

Maggie leaned close and whispered, "What's up with Tania tonight? She's sure in a mood. Don't tell me she's becoming a surly teenager."

I swallowed hard. "Hey, what have you got against

teenagers?" I tried to make it a joke, but I'm not sure it worked, because Maggie looked embarrassed.

"I'm sorry, I didn't mean . . . you know, teenagers are supposed to be sullen, but you're not like that."

I shrugged and blushed, fumbled with my silverware, and dropped my fork. It hit the plate with a loud clank. "Tania's just in a mood tonight." Sometimes I really wish we could tell Maggie about Tania seeing ghosts. It would be nice if I wasn't the only one responsible for my crazy sister. But Maggie didn't believe in ghosts, so she would just think we were making it up. We had reasons why we couldn't tell anyone, even the people who did believe. I always thought having a secret like that would be fun. But it's kind of lonely.

When Maggie turned away, I leaned toward Tania and hissed, "Give it a rest."

She looked at me with her lip trembling, like she was about to cry. "But where is he?"

I opened my mouth, but then saw Madame Natasha staring at us with a kind of hungry look. I said loudly, "Yes, dinner is good. Why couldn't they just call it steak with potatoes?"

Tania catches on quick. She didn't even glance across the table. "Mom says that gateau thing for dessert is chocolate cake."

I said softly, "Don't worry. We'll have time to . . . um, see everything."

When we'd finished dinner, the captain got up and bowed. "In the olden days, the gentlemen would have gone to the smoking room, and the ladies to the ladies' lounge. But tonight, I'll invite you all to join me in the lounge, to hear the story of a disaster that took place on this very boat. How a decent man failed in his duties one dark night, and the accident that led to lives lost. How that poor soul still walks these decks, trying to make amends for his mistake. The ghost of the *Delta Belle*."

The lounge was just as fancy as the dining room. We passed through the ladies' lounge end, which was all delicate curlicue decorations, and paintings of wispy-looking girls in long dresses. The chairs had high backs and embroidered cushions, and looked really uncomfortable. No wonder men went to the smoking room on the other end. It had big solid chairs, dark green carpet, and lots of shiny brass bits. Still fancy, but in a manly way. It was kind of funny, though, because now it had several of those "No Smoking" signs on the wall, looking way too simple and modern. You could separate the two rooms with a partition, but it was pulled back now.

Most of us sat facing Captain Dale. Madame Natasha dragged a big chair next to his, though. She sat stiff and prim, like a queen looking down on her subjects. That's when I noticed the cameras going behind us. They were filming the captain's story, but of course Madame N had to get in on the act if she could.

When everyone was settled, Bruce nodded to the captain to begin. He gazed around a minute, then he tipped back his head and called out, *"Steee-amboat a-comin'!"* I wasn't the only one who jumped.

Captain Dale's eyes twinkled as he looked around at us. "Once upon a time, you could hear that call up and down the rivers of America. The Mississippi, the Missouri, the Ohio rivers. They went from Saint Paul to New Orleans, Montana to Saint Louis. They plied the bayous of Texas and Louisiana, and the rivers, bays, and coasts of the Pacific Northwest and California. Steamboats were how people and goods got around the country. And in those days, every boy wanted to be a steamboat man."

The captain reminded me of a Mark Twain impersonator I'd heard once. I wondered if his accent was real or just put on for show, like his clothes. Either way, it was good entertainment.

"One young man named Henry O'Brien grew up watching the steamboats pass by his riverside town. He dreamed of traveling with them, and his dream came true. He started as a roustabout—a deckhand. He was on call night and day, sleeping among the freight when he could snatch a few minutes. He carried bales, crates, and wood for the boiler, running over the narrow gangplank. It was a hard life—but he was on the river!"

I glanced at Tania to see how she was taking the show. Her eyes were huge, and her face pale and intent. But she wasn't looking at the captain.

I nudged her. "What's up?"

"He's here!"

What? The ghost? Where?" I followed her gaze but saw nothing. My pounding heart slowed in disappointment. Sure, I know Tania sees ghosts, not me—how unfair is that?—but I was hoping that this time would be different.

Someone tapped my shoulder and I jumped. I looked back to see one of the TV crew, a guy named Mick, frowning at me. He put a finger to his lips. I opened my mouth to make a smart remark, then remembered the cameras. I turned around and slumped in my chair.

The captain finished explaining how Henry O'Brien worked his way up to cub pilot, or apprentice, and then pilot. "He had a good job and a lot of responsibility. Steamboats were more dangerous in those days. They were built to be lightweight and fast—safety came a distant third. Boilers exploded, fires ripped through wooden boats in minutes, snags—underwater trees—tore at the fragile hulls. A steamboat pilot had to know every inch of the river—where the sandbars made water too shallow, where fallen trees or sunken boats lurked just under the surface. He had to know the river in sunlight and on cloudy days, by moonlight and on pitch-dark nights. Mark Twain said that a pilot had to learn more than anyone ought to be allowed to know. And he had to learn it all over again every twenty-four hours, because the river kept changing."

I tried to concentrate on the captain's words, to pretend everything was normal. But I kept looking away, to see Tania's tight face, to follow her gaze though I knew I would see nothing. I wished we were alone and she could tell me what she saw.

Captain Dale was talking about one dark night. I wrenched my attention back to him. This story could be important if we were to help the ghost. Or rather, if Tania was to help the ghost, and I was to help her. I wanted to know what I was dealing with. What kind of man had this Henry O'Brien been? What kind of ghost had he become?

"It wasn't the worst section of river," Captain Dale said. "Otherwise, he might not have been alone in the pilothouse. Pilots worked six hours on and six hours off. Maybe he hadn't slept much during his last break. Who knows? Anyhow, he must have fallen asleep. Dozed off, maybe just for a minute." Captain Dale paused and looked around solemnly. "A pilot, in charge of a boat full of passengers, and he fell asleep."

He sighed and shook his head. I wondered if he'd taken acting lessons, or if it came naturally. He was way more convincing than Madame Natasha. She watched him with a screwed-up face, like he was something yucky.

"The ship hit a snag," the captain went on, "a sunken log. Henry O'Brien must have jerked awake at the impact. But by then it was too late. The hull ripped open. Water flooded in. Henry started ringing the bell, the warning signal. Crewmen dragged themselves out of sleep. Passengers ran from their staterooms in their nightclothes, screaming and stumbling in the dark."

Even there in a brightly lit room, I could imagine the scene. Darkness, people running and shouting, the boat tipping as it started to sink. Sliding along the sloping decks, people trying to keep on their feet, not knowing where to go. I swallowed and my throat felt tight. I kind of wished we were back on solid ground.

"Some people panicked and jumped overboard." Captain Dale shook his head. "Few people could swim in those days. A few caught hold of floating pieces of wood. Most drowned. Those who stayed on board fared better. The boat drifted a bit, hit a sandbar, and tipped on its side. A few more people tumbled off. But most held on and scrambled to the highest point. There, they shivered in the night, hoping the boat wouldn't catch fire or explode."

I couldn't hold back any longer. I leaned toward Tania and whispered, "What's he doing?"

She didn't have to ask whom I meant. "He's listening."

Listening to his own story. I shivered. What would it be like, to come back from the grave and hear people talk about you? Especially when they talked about your failure, the lives lost because of you.

"They saw the light of another steamboat coming up the river," the captain said. I think every one of us sat up a little straighter, filled with the hope the passengers must have had. "They called out. Rang the bell for help. The other steamboat tooted its whistle—and kept going. They had a schedule to keep."

His audience gasped, sank back. I heard a sob, and realized it came from my mother.

Captain Dale shook his head sadly. "They waited on through the night. Finally, a chilly dawn broke. Finally, they could see, build a raft of boards, and float down-river to get help. Fifty-two people survived." The captain gazed around the room, as if looking each and every one of us in the eye. "At least seventy people died—no one knows the number for sure, because they didn't keep records of the second-class passengers who slept on the deck. We also don't know exactly when or how Henry O'Brien died that night. But he did, and he's still here."

A horrible moan split the air.

CHAPTER 4

just about jumped out of my skin. Then I realized who was making the sound—Madame Natasha. I guess she felt the captain was getting too much attention, and she wanted to steal the show. It worked. We all gaped at her.

"I feel him," she moaned. "So much guilt . . . so much pain! He wants to make amends."

I swear Captain Dale was trying not to laugh. "Well, that's the story anyway. People have claimed to feel a presence, usually in or around the pilothouse."

Madame Natasha glared at him—she obviously wasn't finished. But he went on cheerfully. "Sometimes people wake in the night, thinking they've heard warning cries. But when they investigate, nothing is wrong."

"Yes . . . yes . . . ," Madame Natasha put her fingers to her forehead. "I hear his voice. . . . He's trying to make up for his failure. . . ."

I leaned over to Tania. "What's he doing now?"

Tania's nose wrinkled. "Staring at her with his mouth open. I wish they'd finish."

Mick poked us from behind and glared. I looked at Tania and jerked my head toward the back of the room. She nodded. We slipped out of our chairs and crept along the wall, careful to stay out of camera range.

Maggie got up as we passed, and followed behind. We all stopped just outside the doors, where we could still see in through the glass panels. "What did you think of that little performance?" Maggie asked.

Tania just stuck out her tongue. I said, "Remember how you told us to be skeptical? Well, with the Madame—it's easy."

"Yeah, I'd bet real money she's a fraud." Maggie stared through the glass in the doors and shook her head. "I can't figure out why Bruce doesn't see that."

"I don't think Mom likes her," I said.

"Your mom's not that dumb," Maggie said.

"Do you think Mom's jealous?" Tania asked. "Bruce couldn't really like that . . . that *freak*, could he?"

My stomach twisted. Bruce wasn't my favorite person, but as stepfathers go, he wasn't that bad. He mostly left us alone. And I thought he made Mom happy.

Maggie gazed into the lounge, frowning thoughtfully. She said in a perfectly serious voice, "I think your mom could take her."

Tania clapped her hand over her mouth, and I let out a snort of laughter. Mean Mick must have ears in the back of his head, because he turned around and glared through the door.

Maggie grinned. "So what are you two up to now, if you've had enough of the, um . . . performance? I bet it's nice up on the top deck."

My heart beat faster. I imagined walking with Maggie in the cool night air, under the stars.

Tania stared through the glass in the doors. She bit her lip and started to fidget. "We, um, we have to . . . We've got . . . " She gave me a pleading look.

"Do you need the bathroom?" I asked.

She rolled her eyes and made faces at me. Fortunately, Maggie was looking into the lounge and didn't notice.

"Looks like the show's over," Maggie said. "I'd better get in there and help with the cameras." She flashed a smile over her shoulder and went inside.

Tania was bouncing like a basketball.

"What?" I asked. "Would you stop freaking out and just tell me?"

"He's coming!" she hissed. "The ghost is coming this way!"

Where?" I winced as I caught myself, once again, king for something I knew I couldn't see. I sighed. So what do you want to do about it?"

"Talk to him! The way he was watching the captain and the fraud, I'm sure he can understand people."

"Fine," I muttered. "Can you just please try to be careful, and maybe not get me in trouble?"

"I just want to help."

"That's what worries me."

Tania whipped around and started walking.

"Hey, where are you going?" I called. "I thought you wanted to—" She was talking as she moved, her head turned to the side. The ghost must have walked right through the door and gone past us—or through us. I felt kind of queasy.

Tania stopped near the railing. I hung back, trying to figure out where to stand. Behind Tania, looking over her shoulder toward a ghost I couldn't see? Or in front of her, so I could see and hear her better? But then I'd be behind the ghost, which felt weird. And what if he moved or turned around, and came right through me? Would I get that freezing-cold thing that Tania got with the last ghost? Or if I couldn't see ghosts, did that mean I couldn't feel them either? I wasn't sure I wanted to find out.

I settled for edging up beside Tania, between her

and where I thought the ghost should be—but not too close to the ghost. Her gaze flew to my face, her eyes bright in the moonlight. "See, Jon, I told you I'd find him! And it's okay, he can understand me. He's . . . he's like Frank, not like Rose."

Good thing, since Rose was the crazy one. That was Tania's way of telling me that she didn't think this ghost was dangerous. I wasn't going to count on her first impressions, though. "Great. So this is Henry O'Brien?"

"Yes. Mr. O'Brien, this is my brother, Jon."

I had this ridiculous urge to hold out my hand to shake. Instead, I nodded toward the blank space where the ghost should be. "Uh, nice to meet you." I felt like an idiot.

"We want to hear your story," Tania said, "and we want to help. What the captain was saying in there, was that all true?" She listened a minute, nodded, listened some more.

"Tania," I muttered, "remember me?"

"Oh, sorry. Mr. O'Brien, my brother can't hear you, so I'll have to tell him what you said." She turned to me. "Captain Dale basically got it right. Mr. O'Brien dozed off when he was on duty and wrecked the ship. He feels responsible for the people who died."

I thought back on the captain's story. "When exactly did he die? I mean, how?"

Tania glanced at the ghost, waited a minute, and then said, "He was trying to rescue somebody, to save just one life. He dove into the water, but he can't swim. Isn't that strange, working on a boat, and you can't swim." She paused, then added, "He says hardly anybody knew how to swim, even the crew. If you fell in the water, you probably drowned."

"Tough line of work," I said.

"I can swim," Tania said.

"I know that—"

"We both can," she went on. "Most kids learn these days." Oh, she was talking to the ghost. That was so hard to get used to.

"So now what?" I asked. "Mr. O'Brien seems like a reasonable guy." That was my way of saying he didn't sound like a maniac. Of course, I didn't have much to go on. At least he seemed to be talking to her like a human being. "So what can we do for him?" I looked vaguely toward where he must be. "What can we do for you?" With luck, we could have this wrapped up by morning, and spend the rest of the trip just having fun.

"I know you feel bad about what happened," Tania said, "but it's over. Can't you move on?"

She frowned. "He said, 'It's all my fault. I have to save them.'"

"A little late for that," I said under my breath.

"Mr. O'Brien, they're all gone. That was a long time ago. Even the people who survived that night have gone on. Everyone who was on the boat that night has . . . has died."

She edged closer to me. "He just keeps repeating, 'I have to save them. I have to save them.'"

"Mr. O'Brien," I said, "that accident was years ago. Almost a century. They're all dead now. There's nothing you can do for them."

"You have to let it go," Tania said. "They've all moved on. It's time for you to move on as well."

She started to reach out a hand, then pulled it back. "He doesn't get it," she whispered. "He thinks there's still something he can do." She bit her lip. She didn't look so happy and confident now, and I groaned inwardly. Of course it wouldn't be easy.

I heard voices behind us. People must be leaving the lounge. "We can't stay here," I hissed at Tania. "Better leave it for now."

"All right. Mr. O'Brien, we'll talk to you later. Don't worry, we'll find some way to help."

I don't know if he hung around or moved off. Tania and I turned together.

And wound up face-to-face with Madame Natasha.

CHAPTER 5

We stared at her. She gave us this creepy smile. "Children! How wonderful to see you again. I hope you've been very well."

Tania and I exchanged a glance and said nothing. I know I couldn't think of anything to say. Madame Natasha had pretty much ignored us when we filmed the last show, except to disagree with Tania's identification of the ghost.

Madame Natasha oozed closer. "I didn't get to know you before, but I've been so looking forward to the chance." She put a hand on Tania's arm, and Tania stiffened. "Such a pretty girl," the fraud gushed. "If I had a daughter, I imagine she'd be just like you. Why, you remind me of myself at your age!"

Tania's face twisted, and I wasn't sure whether to laugh or feel sick.

"I want to know all about you!" Madame N went on. "You're how old now?"

"Um, eleven," Tania stuttered.

"Eleven! A wonderful age. The best age." Madame Natasha gave a dreamy sigh. "Ah, I remember what it was like. The world was so new, so full of . . . interesting possibilities." She gave a smile that was almost a smirk.

Interesting possibilities. The unease that had been dancing around my stomach settled there for good. She meant something by that. She must have heard something we'd said. But what was she suggesting? Was it some condescending grown-up remark, trying to play along in a game she didn't believe? But then, she did believe in ghosts, or said she did. Of course, we knew she couldn't really see them. Why would she think anyone else could?

Madame Natasha lifted a hand and touched Tania's face. Tania flinched, her whole body tight. Don't you hate it when strange grown-ups think they have a right to pet you?

"Such a dear girl," Madame N cooed. "I'm sure we have much to talk about." Tania shot me a pleading glance. I wanted to get away, too, but my mind was blank. I heard voices not too far off. If only someone would come around the corner. I felt like shouting for help, but what would I say when people came?

"You know, being a psychic is a rare and wonderful gift." Madame Natasha stood too close to Tania and stared into her eyes like a snake hypnotizing a rabbit. Tania was pressed back against the railing and couldn't move.

"I can see you have the gift," Madame Natasha purred. "The gift of seeing things that others can't see, of knowing the unknowable." She leaned in even closer. "I could train you, teach you. Guide you. Help you make the most of that gift."

My laugh sounded funny, too loud and ragged. "We don't believe in that garbage." I hoped she didn't hear the shake in my voice. I tried to put on a cocky smile. "Sorry, I know it's your big thing and all. But Tania and me, we're skeptics. We believe in scientific proof, not all this mumbo jumbo."

Madame Natasha glared at me. "People without imagination often can't see things, even things right in front of their faces. But just because you don't have the gift, you should not deny your sister the chance to explore the mysteries."

Tania huffed out a breath, like the spell was broken. She slipped sideways away from Madame N and stood shoulder to shoulder with me. "Jon's right. This is all fun, the TV show and the ghost stories and all that. But it's just a game." She took a breath. "We like to pretend sometimes the ghosts are real. You know, pretend we can talk to them." She gave the sweet, innocent smile that made her look about six years old. "After all, we're just kids."

Madame Natasha stared at us, one hand fisted on her hip. We stared back, meeting her scowl with bland innocence.

She opened her mouth again, then turned her head quickly. People came around the corner, and I sagged with relief. Bruce's voice had never sounded so good.

Madame Natasha turned back with that creepy smile and said softly, "Lovely children." Her gaze focused on Tania. "I'll talk with *you* more later."

Then the others were around us, Bruce, Mom, and Maggie. Tania darted to Mom and hugged her tight. Mom's eyebrows went up, but she settled Tania into her arms and stroked her hair. I felt like I could use a hug myself. Since Mom was busy, Maggie would do. But I just tried to act like nothing strange had happened, and gave a friendly smile. "All done for the night?" My voice croaked a little and I cleared my throat.

Maggie smiled and winked at me. "We got some great footage. The captain is a brilliant storyteller, and of course . . ." Her voice turned silky. "Madame Natasha always knows how to put on a good show."

Bruce grinned, missing the cynicism. "It was brilliant! We've got our second segment right there, a great follow-up to the bit with Madame Natasha coming on the ship. We're halfway through the show, and we have two days left." His eyes focused somewhere in the distance. "I can see an Emmy for this one."

Mom smiled at him. "I hope so. You deserve it."

Maggie grinned at the unusually quiet psychic. "And what does Madame Natasha see?"

The fraud had been frowning, wrapped in her own thoughts. She looked up to see everyone watching her and quickly went back into performance mode. "Oh, yes." She put a hand to her temple and closed her eyes. "I see a glorious future," she murmured. "The fates have arranged for us to be together. To work together, to plumb the mysteries of the invisible. The spirits are pleased and will offer their help."

Bruce watched her hungrily. "How about an Emmy? Do you see an award? It would mean so much to the show. They'd renew us next season for sure, then. People would start to notice." I realized from his expression that he had no interest in Madame Natasha as a woman. He wanted what he thought she offered—success, maybe fame. The chance to prove to skeptics, like my scientist father, that he wasn't just some nut wasting time.

I sighed. Tania and I knew that Bruce was right

about ghosts. Was it wrong of us not to help him? Were we being unfair to keep this secret?

I shook my head. We didn't really have any choice. Tania and I had gone over it all when she first admitted to me that she could see ghosts. Bruce would want to use her gift for the show. Mom would want her to contact our dead sister, and Tania didn't know how to do that. Tania wanted to help the ghosts because she was a sweet kid who hated to see anyone suffer. But she didn't want to be famous, especially not for something that our own father wouldn't believe. She didn't need that kind of pressure.

I looked at her snuggled up to Mom and decided again that my first loyalty was to Tania. She didn't have anyone else, and she wasn't as tough as she pretended. Oh, she was a lot tougher than she looked. But then she'd almost have to be.

I yawned and stretched my arms up. "It's getting late. Maybe we should find our cabins."

"Good idea," Mom said. "I'll come with you and get you settled." She was going to take advantage of Tania's cuddly mood for as long as possible. That meant Tania and I couldn't talk privately, but it might also keep Madame Natasha away.

Tania and I had rooms next to each other. They dropped me at mine and started away. Then Tania turned back, as if she'd just remembered something. She took two quick steps to me, leaned close and whispered, "Tomorrow! I have an idea."

By the time she got back to her cabin door and turned to wave, I'd forced a smile on my face. But inside I was groaning. Did she have to tell me that just before I went to sleep? Imagining Tania's ideas was enough to give me nightmares all night.

CHAPTER
6

I woke to the sound of knocking, rolled over, and buried my head under my pillow. The knocking stopped, and I sighed in relief. It couldn't possibly be morning yet.

After about ten seconds, the knocking started again. I groaned and rubbed my eyes.

The knocking went on. "Just a minute!" I yelled. I sat up and tried to blink away sleep. I found my watch. eight thirty. Why did people have to start the day so early?

I stumbled to the door and opened it. Tania beamed at me. "Morning, sleepyhead!"

I hate morning people. "Go away," I mumbled. "Come back in a couple of hours."

"Don't you want breakfast?"

I hesitated.

"Scrambled eggs, bacon, pancakes, fresh-squeezed orange juice . . ."

"Really?"

She nodded. "We have a lot to do today. You'll need your energy. Better hurry before Mick finishes all the sausages." She grinned at me over her shoulder as she skipped away.

I closed the door and sighed, then started to get dressed.

Most people had finished breakfast already. Mom and Bruce were busy discussing the day's shoot with the rest of the team, over cups of coffee. Tania fluttered around the room, looking, listening, always moving. I filled a huge plate and no one even muttered about healthy eating. It was a good breakfast, almost worth getting up early for, even if Mean Mick did grab the last sausage just as I was reaching for the tongs.

Finally, Tania threw herself into the chair next to me. "Aren't you done yet? Come on, we have things to do."

I eyed her suspiciously as I chewed a mouthful of eggs. "What kind of things?"

She sat up straight, almost bouncing. "I figured out how we can help the ghost!" she hissed.

The sinking feeling started and I sighed. Yeah, I figured as much. "All right, but don't talk about it here." I grabbed two more pieces of bacon as we headed out the door.

Tania practically danced along the passage. She took me to the back of the boat, near the big paddle wheel. We looked around to make sure nobody could hear us.

"It's so easy!" she said. "He wants to prevent a disaster. He won't believe it's too late to fix that other one, so we just have to give him a new disaster."

That sinking feeling finished sinking. "What, you want us to wreck the steamboat?"

"Not *wreck* it," she said, "just let the ghost think it's in danger. We set up a fake accident. He warns people in time or fixes things or whatever. And then he can go on."

On the surface it sounded like a reasonable plan. But I had the feeling that, like the river, a whole lot of snags lurked just under the surface. "And just how are we supposed to stage this disaster? Do you want me to jump in the water and drag a tree in our path? Maybe hit a pilot on the head and steer the boat toward a sandbar?"

Tania rolled her eyes. "Don't make it so complicated. We won't do anything big. We'll just—" She looked around and gestured vaguely with a hand. "Find something to undo. A switch to flip or a dial to turn. Something harmless that looks dangerous."

I pressed my fingertips to my eyes. "Tania. We don't know anything about steamboats. How are we supposed to know what looks dangerous but isn't really?"

She scowled. "We'll figure something out! Look, this

thing back here, it's the paddle wheel, right?" She waved at the big arch of wood that covered the huge rotating wheel. The water churned behind.

"Right."

"That's got to be important."

"Well, yeah, I'd say that if it moves the boat, it's pretty important."

"So, we just have to find a way to do something to it." She leaned over the railing, ignoring the danger signs.

I grabbed her and hauled her back. "Okay, okay, let me." I glanced around. "You keep watch."

I don't know where Tania gets these crazy ideas. The whole boat was designed to keep things safe, to keep stupid passengers from causing problems. All you could really see of the paddle wheel was the protective wood cover. That was probably just as well. I didn't feel like losing an arm.

Finally, I turned back to Tania. "All right, maybe we could loosen some of these bolts. Not too much, because I sure don't want the whole thing falling off. But if we loosen them, maybe that will be enough to make the ghost think there's a problem." And we'd just be messing with the cover, not the wheel itself, so I didn't think we could do any real damage.

Tania peered where I pointed, and nodded eagerly. "All right, great! Let's do it."

"It's not quite that easy," I said. "These are on tight. I'll need a wrench or something."

Tania glanced around. "I bet they have a toolbox in the boiler room."

"Great. You can just walk in there and ask to borrow it."

She lifted her chin. "Fine, I'll get one somehow."

I leaned on the railing as she pranced away. I thought about adding some basic tools—hammer, screwdriver, wrench—to my list of things to bring on these trips. I decided against it. It would only encourage Tania in these crazy ideas.

She came back with a wrench in less than five minutes. I decided not to ask how she got it. That would probably just make me an accessory to a crime. The one I was about to commit already had me sweating.

I turned the wrench over in my damp hands, trying to find an excuse not to use it. "Where's your ghost, anyhow? We can't leave this thing damaged all day."

Tania chewed on her lip. "I know. But we can't let him see us do it either." She shrugged. "I'll find him when we're done."

She made things sound so easy. "Maybe you should—"

Someone came around the corner.

I fumbled the wrench and nearly dropped it on my

foot. When I finally got a grip on it, I shoved it behind my back. My heart was still pounding, and it took a few seconds to focus my vision.

Tania was greeting one of the boat's crew, a black man with long sideburns. He wore baggy dark pants and a loose white shirt of some rough cloth. He grinned and tipped his cap to her.

"It must be wonderful to work on a steamboat," Tania gushed. "You must just love your job."

He waved a hand toward the river. "On a day like this, with blue skies, a fresh breeze, and a nice set of passengers on board? There's nothing better than being a rooster on a steamboat."

Tania's forehead wrinkled. "Rooster?"

"A roustabout. That's what they called deckhands on steamboats. Rooster for short."

Tania laughed. "But I bet you're no chicken!"

I sagged against the railing, letting my heart rate return to normal. I am just not cut out for a life of crime.

"Everything all right back here?"

"Huh?" I looked up to see the rooster studying me. "Oh, yeah, great. Just um . . . looking at the paddle wheel."

He nodded. "Impressive, isn't it? But be careful back here. It's been a long time since we've had anyone fall off the boat, and we don't want to start today."

I swallowed. "Have you really had people fall overboard?"

"Used to happen more in the old days. We have more safety features now. Like this." He patted the wooden dome that covered the paddle wheel. "Most old riverboats didn't have this cover. If you fell off the back, you might have gotten smacked around by the paddles before you drowned."

He smiled. "Down in the lower Mississippi, the roosters used to talk about a giant alligator called Old Al. Said he wore a gold crown and smoked a pipe. When he swished his tail, it made currents to drag a boat off course. When he smoked his pipe, you couldn't see through the fog. And every once in a while, he might pick a roustabout off a steamboat for a snack."

Tania and I stared at him. He must've thought we were impressed by his story, but I just wished he would go away. Tania gazed up with wide eyes and said, "I hope we won't meet anything like that on this trip!"

The rooster grinned back. "You can't get in much trouble these days, so long as you follow the rules and don't do anything stupid."

He glanced at me. I felt like he could see right through me, to the wrench still clutched awkwardly behind my back. But he tipped his hat and said, "Better finish my rounds." He turned the next corner, whistling.

I looked at Tania. "I can't do this. It's stupid. There are too many people around. We'll get caught."

"Fine," she huffed. "Give me the wrench and I'll do it." She held out her hand. The sleeve of her sweater fell away from her thin wrist.

"You're not strong enough."

She stomped her foot. "I am, too! Don't tell me what I can and can't do!"

I tipped my head back and closed my eyes. The sun felt good on my face. *I should just go find a deck chair and spend the day napping. Let Tania take care of herself, if she's so insistent. Let her get in trouble.*

I opened my eyes. "All right, I'll do it. But keep watch. Carefully!"

CHAPTER
7

We checked around the corners, and then I got to work. Unfortunately, there were three places where people might appear. Someone could come out of the passageway on either side of the boat. Or they could come to the back of the second deck, and look over the railing. The best thing Tania could do was to stand close behind me. She could block the view of anyone who appeared, and listen and look carefully to give early warning.

I clenched the wrench in my sweaty hand, hoping it wouldn't slip out and into the water. I hooked it over one of the bolts and pressed hard. Nothing moved. I leaned my full weight onto it. I pushed down for what seemed like minutes. Had it moved just a little? I couldn't even be sure. My hand hurt from gripping the wrench.

It slipped, I was sure of it. I let out a breath. Once

it started, the bolt moved more easily. I gave it one full turn around.

I stood up straight. "There."

Tania turned around to look. "What? Did you do anything?"

"I loosened that bolt!"

She tipped her head to the side and frowned. "It doesn't look loose."

"Trust me, it was a whole lot tighter than that."

She rolled her eyes. "Look, Jon, we need to convince a ghost that this is really a problem. I don't think that's going to do it."

"All right, all right. I'll make it looser."

"And do a couple more," Tania said, "just to be sure."

I groaned and got to work. No way was I going to make things so loose that it might actually cause an accident. But there must have been two dozen bolts, going all the way around the circle of the cover. I didn't think it would hurt to have a few loose ones, for a little while. I just had to make it look good.

Finally, I stepped back. "There, are you satisfied? That's three—"

Tania jabbed her elbow in my back. "Hi, Maggie!" she chirped. "What's up?"

I dropped the wrench. It hit my leg, bounced off the low wall, and clattered on the ground. I dove for it.

Smack! My forehead hit the railing.

I staggered upright, my vision all dark and bright spots.

"Jon? You okay?" Maggie asked.

I turned and leaned casually against the railing, putting my foot over the wrench. Good thing I wear big shoes. "Yeah, fine." I blinked, trying to focus on her, and smiled. "How's it going?"

I saw laughter in her smile. My face burned.

"We'll be landing in a couple of hours," Maggie said. "Bruce wants to film a reenactment, and it will be easier if we're not moving as much. Think about whether you want to watch the filming, or get off and explore the town for an hour."

"Will do!" Tania said.

I nodded, then wished I hadn't. My head throbbed.

Maggie gave a wave and moved on. Tania let out a long breath. "Wow, that was close! She thought you were just trying to be macho and pretend you weren't hurt, so she didn't notice the wrench."

"What luck," I muttered, rubbing my forehead. "Can we get on with this?"

Tania grinned. "I'll go look for Henry O'Brien."

"Great. I'll stay here and make sure the boat doesn't fall apart."

She scurried off. I leaned against the railing and

closed my eyes. The pain in my head faded. I tried to think about what lay ahead. Tania would come back with the ghost. We'd point out the loose bolts like we just happened to notice them. Wait, where was the wrench?

I picked it up. If the ghost saw the wrench, he might wonder what it was doing there. I should hide it. But maybe he would need it to tighten the bolts again. Or we would need it. He probably couldn't do anything physical himself, so he'd have to tell us what to do. I stared at the wrench as if it could give me the answer. Finally, I just shoved it in my pocket and pulled my shirt over the top.

If everything went well, we could be rid of the ghost within half an hour. We could spend the rest of the trip laughing about Madame Natasha making up stories. I leaned back on the railing and felt the sun on my face. Peaceful.

So why couldn't I believe that things would simply go well?

I heard Tania's voice before I saw her. I couldn't quite catch the words, so I wasn't sure if she was talking to the ghost or someone else. I tensed up, waiting for her to come around the corner. My heart beat a little faster.

She appeared, her head turned to one side, talking to nothing I could see. It gave me that same funny jolt every time. I wanted to believe my eyes, almost *had* to believe my eyes. I didn't see anyone there, so no one could be there. Tania had to be playing a game. And yet, I knew it was more than that. I knew she really saw something that I couldn't see. Which of us was right? Which was reality?

She bounced up to me, trying to hide her smile. I shook my thoughts aside.

"I found him," she told me. "I told Mr. O'Brien we saw something strange and needed his help."

I moved aside so she could point out the loose bolts. "Are those supposed to be like that?"

I realized I was holding my breath, waiting for his reaction, and let it out slowly. *Please work,* I thought. *Please let it be this easy.*

Tania took a step back, watching something. I imagined the ghost, Mr. O'Brien, leaning over the railing to look at the bolts. Would he be dressed like the roustabout we'd seen? No, he'd been a pilot. He'd be dressed more like the captain, maybe in a dark jacket and vest. Did he have one of those long mustaches, or a beard? I'd have to ask Tania.

Tania's gaze shifted, so I thought the ghost had straightened. She gave him her best innocent look, big blue eyes wide. "Is that bad? Do you think you can fix it?"

She listened a moment, then her face changed. "It's not . . . We're not playing games." Her eyes shifted to me, then back to the empty space. "We just happened to see it, and thought, you know, we could tell you . . ."

She took a step back, half stumbling, and grabbed the railing for support. Her mouth opened like she was going to scream. I jumped forward, grabbing for her.

The shock hit me in an icy wave. Like breaking through the ice into a frozen pond.

Like dying.

CHAPTER

8

I felt like I was drowning in ice. I couldn't move, couldn't breathe, couldn't think.

And then it was over, and I was on my hands and knees on the deck, gasping for breath.

Tania huddled beside me. "Jon! Jon, are you all right?"

I sat back and leaned against the wall. "What happened?"

Her shoulders hunched up. "You tried to walk right through him."

"Is that what it was like when Rose touched you? When you took her spirit inside of you?" I scrunched into a ball, trying to get warm. "I thought I was going to die."

"It's pretty awful, and you weren't prepared. I guess with Rose I had some warning, some idea of what I was getting into. And I wanted to help her, so that made it okay." Tania sat back and her shoulders relaxed. She managed a smile. "Well, I guess you can't doubt me anymore. Maybe you can't see ghosts, but you sure can feel them."

Heat rose in my face, battling the cold. I had a hard time meeting her gaze. I hadn't realized she knew how much I'd doubted her. I hadn't realized how much I had still doubted her, even when I told myself she had to be telling the truth. I'd wanted proof I could see or hear or feel. Well, I'd gotten it.

I took a deep breath and tried to let go of the cold and fear. "So what the heck happened? I take it our little plan didn't work."

Tania sighed. "Not even close. He guessed it was a trick, or thought we were playing some kind of prank. He got angry, told me how dangerous it was to mess with anything on the boat." She frowned in thought. "I wonder if that was why it was so bad when you tried to walk through him. If the cold is worse when he's angry or upset."

"I don't think I want to test all the possibilities," I muttered.

Tania laughed. "Why, Jon, where's your spirit of scientific investigation?"

"In cold storage."

We sat quietly for a minute, just listening to the

water splashing behind the boat. The air had a fresh tangy smell, with just a hint of something mechanical, like grease.

Tania sat with her knees drawn up and arms folded over them. She rested her chin on her arms, her eyes clouded with thoughts. Now that it was over, I was kind of glad I'd felt the ghost. Glad I understood something of what she went through. Even glad I had her for a sister. If I'd had a choice of who to take on these trips, I might have chosen one of my buddies back home, or a cute girl. Instead I had my annoying, difficult little sister. But she was all right. I was even starting to admire her.

Tania lifted her head and shook herself with a sigh. She saw me watching her. "What?"

"Nothing."

She frowned. "I don't know what to do next—"

"That's a relief."

She stuck out her tongue. "Don't worry, I'm sure I'll come up with another plan soon. Right now, maybe I'd better go find Mr. O'Brien and try to make up to him. Convince him we're his friends. Then maybe we'll figure out something when they shoot the reenactment."

I nodded and stretched. "Sounds good. I'd better tighten these bolts again."

"All right," Tania said, springing up. "We'll catch up later."

I sat there while she bounced away, then slowly rose. I felt like an old man. I hoped I'd have a chance to relax for a while before the next adventure. Maybe I could go up to the pilothouse and watch the pilots. Just do regular stuff.

I pulled out the wrench and leaned over the railing. A couple of quick twists would have everything back to normal.

One tightened. Two tightened.

A voice growled behind me. "Just what do you think you're doing?"

I jumped. The wrench leaped from my grasp, bounced off the paddle wheel cover and flew through the air. It dropped into the water with barely a splash among the ripples of our wake.

I turned slowly, already knowing who I would see.

Mean Mick glared at me. "You are in big trouble, kid."

CHAPTER

I groaned. Perfect, just perfect. Just what I needed to make this day even better.

I tried to ignore the jumpy feeling in my stomach. Tried to pretend the sweat beading on my face was just from the warm sun.

I forced a smile, trying to imitate Tania's wide-eyed innocent look. "Hello. What's up?"

"Don't take that tone with me. I saw what you were doing, you young vandal."

I let my eyebrows go up. "Vandal? I don't understand." I stared at him, trying to keep my expression bland and friendly. I don't think he was buying it. He kept scowling. But then, I'd never seen him do anything else, so it was hard to say what that meant.

"You had a wrench in your hand, and you were loosening those bolts."

"I was doing nothing of the kind!" I tried for injured

innocence. I should have known better. People never believe me when I'm telling the truth.

"Ha!" He grabbed my arm. "We'll just see what Bruce has to say about this."

I tried to twist away but couldn't loosen his grasp. He started walking, dragging me behind. I gave up the fight and followed. If he was going to haul me in front of Bruce as a vandal, at least I'd go calmly, with pride, not struggling like I was guilty.

It was hard to stay calm when he dragged me past a roustabout and a couple of the TV crew members. It was harder when I saw Madame Natasha and the captain ahead. It was almost impossible when he shoved me up to Bruce, Mom, and Maggie.

"I found this young devil vandalizing the boat!" Mick was practically yelling, full of righteous indignation.

Everyone turned to stare at him. Then their gazes shifted to me. I felt my face flaming, and couldn't help trying to twist my arm out of his grasp. I probably looked guilty as sin.

Finally, Mom spoke. "Mick, we're busy here. If you have a problem with my son, see me privately. Later." I had never before appreciated that steely tone in her voice. I wanted to hug her.

But Mick wasn't so easily swayed. "This concerns everyone," he said pompously. "The whole boat." He looked around, making sure he had everyone's attention. Madame Natasha, the captain, and several other people drifted up. "I saw him loosening bolts on the paddle wheel."

This got an even longer silence, with everyone staring. I straightened up, trying to look dignified. "You can let go of me now," I said coldly. "Where do you think I'm going to run?"

Mick hesitated, frowning like I'd asked him to give up some great treasure. Finally, he dropped his hand.

The roustabout who'd seen us at the back of the boat came up and whispered something to Captain Dale. The captain said something back, and the roustabout disappeared. That made me nervous, but I tried to ignore them and stay cool.

"I was just leaning over the railing to look at the paddle wheel. I don't know what old Mick here thinks he saw, but I wasn't doing anything wrong."

"He had a wrench!" Mick said. "He was unscrewing a bolt. I saw him!"

I spread my hands wide. "What wrench? I'm not carrying anything. You can search me."

"You threw it over the side!" Mick sputtered. "Littering—polluting the river —"

Mom closed her eyes and pinched her nose between thumb and fingers. "Mick, we appreciate your concern

59

over the safety of the boat." She glared at him and added, "And the moral behavior of my children. But I hardly think my son is a vandal."

Mick gazed around at the other faces. Bruce was frowning, but he just looked confused. Madame Natasha watched us coolly, as if above such petty things. Captain Dale stood at ease, without judgment. Maggie stepped up beside me and gave my arm a quick squeeze. For some reason, that made my eyes moist and I had to swallow hard.

Mick seemed baffled that they didn't automatically believe him. Maybe I should have felt sorry for him, since he was actually telling the truth, at least as he saw it. But I didn't.

I started to relax. I might get away with this after all.

Then the roustabout came back. He and the captain exchanged a glance, and the captain nodded. The roustabout took off his cap and faced the group. My stomach started sinking even before he spoke.

"My apologies, ma'am, sir." He nodded to Mom and Bruce. "I saw the boy and his sister at the back of the boat earlier. He was holding something behind him, kind of secret-like." He shot me a glance and gave a little shrug. "I just went back to look, and somebody was messing with the bolts, sure enough. The paint's a little scratched around two of them, though they're on snug. One was loose, though. I didn't find a wrench, but one is missing from the toolbox."

The faces turned to me, and I didn't like the expressions on them now. I felt my face burning and wanted to sink into the ground.

"See! See!" Mick was practically hopping up and down. "I told you. I know what I saw."

Mom looked at me with hurt and confusion in her eyes. "Jon?"

I fought to hold back tears. My voice came out in a shaky whisper. "I'm not a vandal. That's all I can say."

I didn't notice when Tania had joined us, but she was there now, her face twisted in distress. "He's not! He wouldn't!" She grabbed Mom's arm. "You know he wouldn't."

"Well, yes, but . . ." Mom looked like she was about to cry. She stepped closer to Bruce, and he put an arm around her. He looked almost as upset, but I think he was worried about her, not me.

Tania turned to me. She opened her mouth again, but I gave a little shake of my head. She couldn't help me. Anything she might say would just throw some of the blame on her, and she'd be in trouble, too.

The captain took a step forward. "If I might make a suggestion?"

Mom and Bruce turned to him with obvious relief. "We'd be grateful for your help," Bruce said. I don't think he wanted to discipline me any more than I wanted it.

Captain Dale nodded at me. "Since there's some question about the young man's actions, perhaps a lesson in responsibility is what he really needs. He can spend the rest of the trip working for me, and helping out the boat's crew. If he's innocent, hard work can't do him any harm. If he's guilty, he'll learn to respect this boat." I thought I caught a twinkle in his eyes. "And either way, we'll keep him too busy to get into more trouble."

Mom and Bruce nodded, babbling their agreement. Tania and I exchanged a long look. She gave me a small, sympathetic smile. Part of me knew I'd gotten off easy. Helping the boat's crew, learning how things worked—that was more like a gift than a punishment. But another part of me still burned with humiliation.

I risked a glance at Maggie. She was studying me so intently I had to look away again. She hadn't looked angry, just . . . like she was trying to figure something out. It could be worse anyway. I couldn't bear it if she hated me.

"Lucas," the captain said to the roustabout, "why don't you take this young fellow down to the boiler room and put him to work. Send him up to me after we dock."

The roustabout nodded, and I started after him with a sigh. He was ahead of me in the passage when someone grabbed my arm. I turned to see Tania. "I'm sorry, Jon!"

I just shrugged.

Tania glanced back, then leaned close and hissed, "I'm afraid Mr. O'Brien heard the whole thing! Now he really believes you're a troublemaker. You'd better watch out."

The roustabout had turned back to wait for me. I looked down at Tania and muttered, "Watch out for a ghost I can't see? How am I supposed to do that?"

She lifted a hand in a helpless gesture. "I don't know. I don't know what to do now. We've just made things worse."

CHAPTER
10

Lucas rapped on the boiler room door, then led the way inside. The temperature went up twenty degrees. The whole room seemed to vibrate, with a hum like a thousand bumblebees.

The boiler room was filled with pipes, big and small. I saw half a dozen things that looked like clocks, but with different kinds of numbers, hanging from the walls. A black steering wheel was attached to a thick white pipe that rose through the ceiling. I guessed the wheel controlled how much steam went up, since they sure weren't steering from down here. Smaller pipes ran around the room, with smaller shutoff wheels.

Two men looked up and greeted us. "Brought you a new helper," Lucas said.

One of them frowned and scratched his head. He had red hair, not dyed crimson like Madame Natasha's, but that carroty-orange color and the freckles to go with it. "Mite puny, isn't he?"

I opened my mouth to protest, but wasn't sure what to say. Neither of the men were tall, but they had muscles like comic book superheroes. If they got that way by working in the boiler room . . . well, I didn't want to make an even bigger fool of myself by pretending I could do things I couldn't.

I cleared my throat and said, "Give me a job, and I'll do my best."

The redheaded man laughed and held out his hand. "All right, put her there." I tried to shake with a firm grip, but he just about broke all the bones in my hand. And I don't even think he was doing it on purpose.

"That's Cleavon," Lucas said. "And this is Miguel." Both men had loose white shirts and dark baggy pants like Lucas, but their shirtsleeves were rolled up and they weren't wearing caps. With Miguel's long, drooping mustache and Cleavon's bushy red sideburns, they had that old-fashioned look.

"Do you have to dress that way?" I asked without thinking. Then I thought it might sound rude, so I rushed on. "I mean, everyone looks like they're out of the past. The captain, especially. Is it like a rule?"

"It keeps the tourists happy," Lucas said with a shrug.

"Yep, it's all about tourism nowadays," Cleavon said. "Not like the old days, when rivermen were kings."

"Yeah," Lucas said, "and when I would have been a slave, with my wages paid to my master."

"And when a boilerman was lucky to live to thirty," Miguel added. "Me, I like having pressure gauges and safety valves."

Cleavon just laughed. "All right, so change ain't all bad. But you fellows sure take the fun out of complaining."

"Never seems to stop you."

"Wait a minute," I said. "I thought this boat was from the 1920s." I may not be great in history, but I knew slavery had ended way before that.

"She was built in 1920," Lucas said, "but our costumes are from the 1850s. That was the height of the riverboat era, and that's what people think of—Mark Twain, *Life on the Mississippi*. That's what draws the tourists." He shrugged. "The boat was totally rebuilt anyway. The engines are modern. The decorations in the dining room and lounges are based on pictures of older steamboats. It's more like theater than history."

"But she still has the old spirit," Cleavon insisted.

She had an old spirit, all right. I imagined Henry O'Brien haunting the boat all those years, as she lay rotting, then got pulled out of the water and totally rebuilt.

Lucas clapped me on the shoulder. "I'm off. Jon, if

you can survive these fellows until lunchtime, you'll have worked off all your sins." He left us with a wave.

I was glad he hadn't told the men that I was being punished for vandalism. I was even more grateful that Cleavon and Miguel didn't ask what had brought me there. Maybe they thought I was interested in working on a steamboat someday. Anyway, they showed me around. The boilers were covered with white insulation. Pipes went everywhere, with dials and gauges and knobs. A more modern panel with plastic buttons showed that they had updated some things.

Miguel pointed out the huge iron pipes that rose up through the ceiling. "These are the chimneys you see up top. We feed the furnace, steam pressure builds up in the boilers. It moves a long rod on a piston, and that turns the paddle wheel at the back of the boat."

I'd hoped they'd let me shovel coal into the furnace, but it turns out steamboats use fuel oil these days. It was all a matter of adjusting levers and things. They explained the gauges and valves, but wouldn't let me touch the controls.

Heat radiated from the boiler, and sweat drenched my back. I wiped my arm across my forehead and backed away.

Suddenly, the sweat went cold, like someone dropped an ice cube down my back. I shivered, then spun around to look behind me. The heat of the boiler warmed my back, but my front went cold.

Miguel nodded solemnly. "Henry O'Brien, he keeps his eye on you."

I looked from him to Cleavon. "You mean it? Henry O'Brien—the ghost—you've felt him before?"

Cleavon laughed. "He keeps us in line. Don't think about nodding off, or you'll get a cold blast to wake you up."

"Some say it's just cool breezes, maybe coming through cracks," Miguel said.

"And some say we're cracked!" Cleavon cackled.

"Whatever it is, you get used to it," Miguel said. "The cold is good, when it's so hot in here."

I nodded, trying to take it as casually as they did. It was nice to see tough guys like this believing in ghosts, even feeling friendly toward one. But it wasn't so nice knowing that Henry O'Brien was looking over my shoulder. Tania had said he would, but it was different to feel it. What would he do if I made a mistake?

"Lots of ghost stories on the river," Cleavon said. "There's supposed to be a whole ghost boat, down toward Baton Rouge. The river made a huge horseshoe bend, but during one big storm, it washed out a new channel and the horseshoe started to dry up. A pilot came down in the dark and rain. Couldn't see a thing.

He scraped across a sandbar. Lightning flashed just in time to show him a snag ahead. Nothing was where it should be."

Cleavon rocked back on his heels and grinned. "The pilot started to curse. Cursing was practically a sport in them days. He said he would fight his way out, no matter what the powers threw at him."

"Not a wise thing to say," Miguel said solemnly.

Cleavon shook his head, still smiling. "They say he's still there, still trying to get out. On dark, rainy nights, you might see the steamboat, shining with a faint blue light. You might even hear the pilot, still cursing as he tries to find his way out."

I couldn't tell if they really believed, or were just telling stories. The year before, I would have figured it was just a tall tale. Now I couldn't tell. What would Tania see, if she went to the right spot?

"Time to oil the parts," Cleavon said. He grabbed an oilcan with a long nozzle and started squirting drops of oil on all the pistons and things, as they moved. "We have to oil it all by hand every thirty minutes."

He went over dozens of parts. I wanted to help, but figured I'd just make a huge mess trying to hit all those moving targets. A few bells rang, and Miguel turned some dials. Cleavon crossed the room to check a panel with a digital display. He waved me over, and explained what he was doing. I only followed a little of it.

The guys talked about the old days, when people didn't understand steam pressure very well, and boats didn't have those gauges.

"An engineer had to go by feel back then," Cleavon said. "Figure out by sound and vibration when the boilers were running dry or building up too much steam. An engineer had to trust his instincts."

"And that's why they had so many explosions," Miguel added.

Cleavon nodded. "There ain't too many old boats like this still on the rivers. Most of 'em blew up in boiler explosions or got tore apart on snags and sandbanks, and left to rot."

"Most of the steamboats out there today aren't more than thirty or forty years old." Miguel affectionately patted the wall. "This one had to be almost completely rebuilt, after years of decay. New boilers and everything, of course, because we don't burn wood or coal anymore. But she's still a historic treasure, she is."

Old enough to come with a ghost, I thought.

I was getting along with the guys great. I didn't mind the work, or the heat and the noise. I could've spent all day in there.

Then the door opened without so much as a knock. Mean Mick stepped in.

I think I groaned aloud. In that noisy room, no one noticed. Miguel and Cleavon both stepped toward Mick. "No passengers allowed in here," Miguel said.

Mick looked around with his superior smirk. "I'm just checking on the boy there. I wanted to make sure you're keeping a close eye on him. Don't let him get into any more trouble."

I felt myself going red as Cleavon and Miguel glanced back at me. I wanted to sink into the floor.

"He hasn't been any trouble," Miguel said.

"A darn nice kid," Cleavon added.

Mick's face puckered like he smelled something bad. "That's what he'd like you to think. But he's a vandal. He was caught!"

I couldn't take it anymore. Here I was, trying to help Tania, trying to help a ghost, and Mick had to go around getting me in trouble. "Why can't you just leave me alone—"

I took two fast steps forward, dodging around Miguel. Then I slammed into a wall of cold.

I staggered back and flung out an arm. My hand hit something. I grabbed it for support, then realized it was a huge fire extinguisher—almost as tall as me—that stood in the corner. Before I got my balance, I felt it start to fall.

CHAPTER
11

I think Miguel and Cleavon both yelled. Before I really knew what was happening, Cleavon had the fire extinguisher back in place, and I was across the room by the door, with Miguel's hand on my arm.

"See? See?" Mick demanded, almost dancing with joy. "I told you he was a troublemaker."

Cleavon turned on him, with his shoulders hunched and hands clenched in fists. "Out!" he roared.

Mick froze with his mouth open. Then he spun and went through the door, muttering, "The thanks I get for trying to help . . ."

Miguel still had a hold of my arm, and his grip was starting to hurt. The vibrations were making me queasy and my eyes stung. I swallowed hard as the men looked at me. "I'm sorry. I didn't . . . It was just . . ." Then I remembered that they knew about the ghost, and believed in him. "It was Henry O'Brien—the cold—it surprised me."

Miguel dropped his hand and nodded. "He thought you were going to fight. He doesn't like fighting. It causes accidents."

A bell rang, but outside the room, not one of the signal bells to the engineers. Cleavon ran a hand over his face. "If you ask me, that's plenty of excitement for one day. They're calling the passengers to lunch. You go on now."

I hesitated. I didn't want to leave like that, in disgrace. But I could hardly demand they let me stay. Finally, I said, "Shall I come back after lunch? I'd like to help."

Miguel shook his head. "Don't bother."

My heart sank, but then Cleavon added, "Ain't nothing for you to do here. Captain sent you here, he just figured you'd find it interesting." He thumped my shoulder so hard I staggered. "Captain won't have no liars and vandals working on his boat. So if he put you to work, you must be all right."

I was so grateful, I couldn't speak. I just smiled.

"Besides," Miguel added, "we remember what it was like to be a boy. You get in a scrape now and again, doesn't mean you're bad."

They waved me out of the room, and I headed to lunch. I made sure I had a seat far away from Mick, and told Tania everything that happened. She had some really choice things to say about Mick, and that cheered me up. I'd have to remember the phrase *beetle-brained bozo*. Might come in handy someday.

An hour later, I was in the pilothouse with Captain Dale and the pilot, Mr. Hendrickson. It was a small room, just a couple of paces across. The big wheel was at the front, and a couple of leather-covered benches along the back wall. You could look out the windows at the river all around. I wished I had a better reason for being there, but even so, it was pretty cool. I felt like I'd stepped back in time, and was one of the rivermen from the 1800s. I even wished—it's kind of embarrassing, but it's true—I even wished I had some old-fashioned clothes, like the rest of the crew, and one of those soft hats.

"Make yourself comfortable," the captain said. "Mr. Hendrickson was just about to ask for some more speed."

The pilot moved a lever, and some bells rang. A minute later, the responding bells rang from the engine room. Cleavon and Miguel had heard the signal and responded.

"I can't believe you still use those bells," I said. "Wouldn't it be easier to use cell phones or walkie-talkies?"

"Not really," Captain Dale said. "Once you know this system, it's quick and easy. This tube lets us speak to the men in the boiler room, in an emergency—though it's almost impossible to hear down there, with all the noise, so we hardly use it. The bells get their attention, and the dial down there moves in response to this one to show what we want."

The captain gestured toward the instruments mounted near the ceiling. Several TV screens showed different displays. "We have a few modern conveniences. We no longer have to have a man at the front of the boat, dropping a line to test the depth, and yelling out the soundings. But on this boat, we mostly try to do things the old way. We want to be authentic."

Since they were pretty much ignoring the gadgets mounted by the ceiling, it all looked simple enough. Easier than driving a car, in fact, because you didn't have any pedals—or much traffic. "So all you do is tell the men below to go faster or slower, and then you steer?"

Captain Dale chuckled. "Sounds easy, doesn't it? But where do you steer?"

I frowned and looked out the window. "Well, I guess I'd try to stay to the middle of the river. I mean, unless another boat was coming or something."

"Now that would be simple. But the river isn't always deepest in the middle." He talked about sandbars and snags and other hazards, about rocks and rapids, wide spots and narrow channels.

I nodded, trying to look as mature and responsible as possible. I wanted to ask if I could take the wheel, just for a minute. But I figured he didn't trust me, if he believed Mick. I'd just have to do everything they asked, quick and well. I promised myself that by the time the trip was over, they'd see that I was all right, and that Mick had to be wrong. Well, okay, he wasn't wrong about me doing something to the bolts. But he was wrong about *me*.

"Being a riverboat pilot is a lot of responsibility," Captain Dale said. "They say there are fourteen ways to kill a steamboat, from fires and boiler explosions to hitting snags or rocks or ice. One time a steamboat caught fire at a dock in Saint Louis. The fire spread, and wiped out twenty-three boats and fifteen city blocks. You can't let up your guard for a second or you could run into trouble—like Henry O'Brien."

I felt a sudden chill, like the temperature in the room dropped ten degrees. The hair on the back of my neck stood up, but I tried to shake off the feeling. Just my imagination, thinking about that ancient accident.

"Come take the wheel for a minute, lad," the captain said. Mr. Hendrickson stood aside.

I wiped my palms on my jeans and stepped up to the huge wheel. The bottom went down into the floor and the top rose to chest height. Spokes came out from the wheel every six inches, for handholds. I grabbed a couple and stared ahead at the river.

"We're in a wide place now," Captain Dale said from behind my shoulder. "Try turning the wheel to see how she responds. You can't run into anything here."

I nodded, my eyes still straight ahead. I took a deep breath and turned the wheel slightly. I didn't notice any change. I turned it more. At first I didn't think it had done anything, but then I noticed we were aiming a little to the left. I turned the wheel to the right, and felt the boat respond. It was slow—you couldn't make sharp turns—but smooth. I grinned at the captain and he smiled back.

A cold breeze chilled my neck. I had this awful feeling the ghost was going to sneak up and grab me with that icy shock. What would the captain think if I suddenly collapsed, shivering and numb? I'd look like a wimp and a weirdo, as well as a vandal.

I swallowed hard and tried to tell myself it was just the wind. A couple of the side windows were open.

Captain Dale let me steer for about ten minutes. For a while, I forgot about the ghost. I was just working on the river.

"You're doing well," the captain said. "But don't you start thinking it's always this easy! The accident records prove otherwise. Henry O'Brien was hardly the only case of human error. A lot of the engineers weren't well trained. And sometimes the pilots got into races on the river."

I looked out the window as the banks drifted slowly by. "You mean a couple of steamboats would have, like, a drag race on the river?" It seemed funny, like a couple of little kids trying to race across a pool by dog-paddling.

"They would race between cities. It might take a couple of days, but the owner of the fastest boat would be renowned, and would get more passengers for the next trip."

I laughed. "That sounds pretty fun."

The cold seemed to clamp on the back of my neck. Shivers ran down to my toes and back up again. I couldn't control my arms or legs.

I guess I made Henry O'Brien mad.

CHAPTER
12

I wanted to scream at the ghost, but of course I couldn't. I could only wait and try to keep control.

Captain Dale stepped up beside me. Fortunately, he was gazing out the window, not at me. "A dangerous kind of fun. They'd tie the safety valves closed and get the boilers going full blast. Sometimes it wasn't the fastest boat that won, but simply the one that didn't blow up. Thousands of passengers lost their lives in races. Now we kill each other with cars when we're not careful. Speed isn't always the best goal."

"Right," I gasped. "No racing. Dangerous. Safety first."

Captain Dale turned and cocked an eyebrow at me. Fortunately, Henry O'Brien backed off. I could straighten up and give the captain a smile, though I still felt like someone had dropped a bag of ice cubes down my back. I'd have to watch what I said.

"Now we're coming up to an underwater sandbar," the captain said. "See if you can spot it."

I gazed at the river ahead, not sure what I was looking for. How did you see something underwater?

Something red flashed by in the corner of my vision. It was on the boat, not in the river, and obviously not a sandbar. But I wondered what it was.

There it was again. This time I recognized Madame Natasha's red hair. She was on the deck below, darting forward and then ducking back. She seemed furtive, sneaky. What was she doing? She headed toward the back of the boat.

"See there, how the water changes color?"

"Um." I forced my attention back to Captain Dale and the river ahead. "You mean where it looks kind of white there?"

"Yes. That's the kind of thing you have to look out for. The river flows differently over low ground."

"I see." I wanted to turn around to look for Madame Natasha again. I forced myself to look ahead. "So you go around places like that?"

The captain gently turned the wheel, and the boat moved a little farther out into the river. "Yes. But you have to keep an eye on the other side as well. There might be a snag, maybe a log under the water. They've done a lot to clean up the river. Dams keep the water at an even depth. They haul out snags and other hazards. Still, you never know when a new tree might tumble in."

"Uh-huh."

Captain Dale nodded toward the wall. "That chart there shows the permanent hazards, like rocks."

Finally, an excuse to turn around. I walked over to the chart and pretended to look at it. I leaned toward the side window and glanced out, looking for that red hair. I didn't trust that woman at all. It was frustrating to be stuck up here while she wandered around, maybe causing trouble for Tania.

As soon as I thought of Tania, her head popped up on the stairway. She approached the pilothouse with a timid smile and tapped on the door frame. I gazed past her. Madame Natasha was peeking up the stairs. She saw me looking and ducked back down.

"Um, captain?" Tania said. "I hope I'm not interrupting. I just wanted to see how Jon was doing."

Captain Dale waved her in. "You're welcome here, child. I'm just learning your brother the river." The captain winked at me. "And when I say I'll learn a man the river, I mean it. I'll learn him or kill him."

Tania and I stared at him. The captain burst out laughing. "Don't worry, it's just a quote from Mark Twain. Something his captain told him when he was in training. Did you know that *mark twain* is a river term? It means two fathoms. In shallow water, the pilot would have a man drop a line to test the depth. The man would call out mark twain, mark three, or whatever. Samuel Clemens took the name Mark Twain from his time as a riverman."

"That's cool," I said. These people had Mark Twain on the brain.

Captain Dale showed Tania around. I carefully turned my back on the stairway. I gave it about thirty seconds, then glanced back quickly. Madame Natasha's red hair dropped out of sight again. What was she up to? I needed to get Tania aside for a private talk.

Captain Dale patted her shoulder. "We're taking good care of your brother, don't you worry."

"He really isn't a vandal," she said with the wide, sincere eyes. "I hope you don't believe what that awful man said."

The captain's mustache twitched up. "Don't you worry, dear. I make my own judgments about a man."

That made me feel kind of good. He'd actually called me a man. At least I think so. Maybe he was just talking about Mick.

We neared a small town. "We'll land up here," Captain Dale said. He smiled down at Tania. "Better give them a blast on the whistle, child. Grab that red rope across the ceiling. Hold on tight and pull down slowly. Give it about five seconds."

Tania did as he said. The sound of the whistle started slow, then built up to that wonderful, low *Whooooo!* Tania grinned at the captain. I couldn't believe I actually felt a little jealous.

Mr. Hendrickson eased the boat close to land. There wasn't any dock, just grass dropping off to a steep bank. The captain stepped out the door and hollered over the railing. "Get out the head line and stern line! Tend to the fenders. Swing the stage to starboard."

I rushed out onto the little deck and leaned over the railing. Below, two roustabouts jumped onto land and tied up the boat with thick ropes. A few people on shore waved, and I raised my hand to them. I ducked back into the pilothouse, smiling.

"We're here for a couple of hours," Captain Dale said. "Nothing's happening up here, so you can go watch the filming if you like. Come back when we head out again."

I saluted. "Aye, aye, captain!"

Tania thanked the captain and we left. I stopped her out on the deck. "What's Madame Natasha doing? I think she's following you."

"I keep seeing her, but every time I turn around, she jumps out of sight. Or else she leans against something and looks into the distance, as if she's not paying any attention to me at all. I can hardly tell her to stop; she'd just deny it. Anyway, I don't even want to talk to her."

We crept closer to the stairway and looked down. Sure enough, Madame Natasha was casually leaning on the railing near the bottom of the stairs. I pulled Tania back. "I don't like it. She's up to something."

Tania scrunched up her nose and shrugged. "Obviously, but I don't know what we can do about it."

"Just be careful. She seems to know, or thinks she knows, that you can talk to ghosts. Maybe she's waiting for you talk to Mr. O'Brien again."

"Well, I won't be doing that. He seems to be staying in the pilothouse. He's been watching you."

It was bad enough having live people looking over my shoulder, waiting to see if I'd do something wrong. But to have a ghost watching and judging me? That was just creepy. "I hate this," I said. "It's not fair that he can see me and I can't see him."

Tania gave a little smile. "I guess it's true what they say—life isn't fair. I'd stay if I could, and tell you what he's doing, but . . ."

I shook my head. "No, that's okay. I have to do this on my own." I took a deep breath and set my shoulders. "As long as I don't screw up, or do anything that makes him think I screwed up, I should be all right. Maybe he'll even start to trust us again."

Tania grinned. "Is that what they call positive thinking? Anyway, let's go watch the show."

CHAPTER
13

As we headed down the stairs, I wondered if the ghost was following. Did he understand why we were here, with cameras and a self-proclaimed psychic? What would he make of it all, these things he'd probably never seen when he was alive?

We went to the lower deck and sat on a long box that said LIFE PRESERVERS on the side. The crew bustled about. Maggie glanced over from across the deck. She gave a brief wave, but didn't smile. Mick broke off from saying something to her, looked at me, and glared. Heat rose in my face. I had almost forgotten I was a vandal. But of course, Mick would never forget. Would Maggie?

"Here comes Mr. O'Brien," Tania said.

I looked around. Of course it didn't do any good. "What's he doing?"

"Watching."

"Watching what? Them, or me?"

Tania smiled. "He's mostly watching Bruce right now. Trying to figure out what's going on, I suppose."

Since I couldn't see the ghost, I watched Bruce, too. He was getting his face powdered. It looked really weird to see them putting makeup on a grown man, but I guess that's all part of show business.

Madame Natasha was sitting in a deck chair. Her hands rested on the arms, with the palms turned upward and her thumbs touching her middle fingers, like people do in yoga. I guess she was trying to look meditative, but she kept opening her eyes and giving Tania long looks.

Mom rushed around, making sure the cameras were set up in the right places. Some of the boat crew watched. Finally, Mom called out, "All right, we're set! Mr. Simpson, you know what to do, right?"

A man stepped forward. I'd assumed he was one of the boat's crew, since he was wearing old-fashioned clothes, like Captain Dale, with a vest, jacket, and cap. But I hadn't noticed him before. "Who's that?" I whispered.

"He's an actor," Tania said. "He's playing Mr. O'Brien."

"Shouldn't they be shooting this up in the pilot-house?"

"Later, when it's dark, they'll do the part where he falls asleep. They just want to do some opening stuff now. They're having the real captain play the part of the old captain, since he's such a good actor. And the crew members can be the crew, since they're in costume. Maggie checked all this out ahead of time, of course. I guess part of the appeal was that they wouldn't have to fly out a whole bunch of actors. They could just use the people already here. They're used to putting on a show for the tourists."

"Everyone quiet now," Mick called out. He turned to scowl at Tania and me. "Quiet on the set. Quiet!" Everyone had fallen silent after his first shout, but of course he liked to be bossy.

They filmed Captain Dale greeting the fake Henry O'Brien and welcoming him on board. Tania leaned close and whispered, "Mr. O'Brien is really paying attention now. I guess he heard his name. I wonder what he thinks of it all."

The captain talked about how dangerous the river was because of recent flooding. I wondered who had written the script and if it was anything like what had really happened back then.

Tania put a hand over her mouth to hide her giggles. "Mr. O'Brien is checking out the cameras! I don't think he knows what to make of them."

I looked where she was looking, though I didn't really expect to see anything. One of the cameramen jerked his head up. He looked over the camera, then bent to look through it again. He made some adjustments, looked up, and waved to get Mom's attention.

"Cut!" she said. "Stefan, is something wrong?"

"The camera's gone all foggy." He came around to look at the lens from the front. "It's like it frosted over. I don't get it. We didn't have a big temperature change or anything. It was all right a minute ago."

Mom and Maggie came over to study the camera. Maggie's shoulders went up and she wrapped her arms around herself. "Brrr, I just got a chill. Maybe the weather's changing, and that's what did it."

I started to chuckle, then turned it into a cough when I saw Mean Mick looking at me. If I looked amused, he'd probably think the problem was my fault.

"What's the ghost doing now?" I hissed.

Tania's eyes danced. "He's going over to look at that actor."

The fake Henry O'Brien was talking to the captain and Bruce. "So tonight, when we're filming up top, I'll fall asleep at the wheel."

"Ohh, the ghost doesn't like that!" Tania said. "He's getting agitated."

"The captain will have to show me what to do," the actor went on. "We want the boat to come to a sudden halt, right? Or should I just fake that part, pretend to be jolted?"

"Just pretend," Captain Dale said. "Easier and safer that way."

"Then I'll jump up and run out. You'll have people yelling and screaming, right?"

Bruce nodded. "We'll get everybody to pitch in, especially the women and my stepdaughter. Women and children screaming should be dramatic." He twitched suddenly and glanced over his shoulder. "The breeze is picking up."

Tania bit her lip and I smothered a snort. Poor Bruce. He spent his life tracking ghosts, and couldn't even tell when one was right next to him.

"It's a great part," the actor said. "Neither a hero nor a villain. I always like the complex ones." He got really theatrical. "Oh, what have I done!" he said, thumping his chest. "Destroyed the boat and killed all the passengers!" He put a hand to his brow. "I shall throw myself over the side and drown in my misery." He dropped his hand, laughing.

His eyes went wide and he froze in place.

"Oh, no," Tania gasped. "The ghost has him!"

CHAPTER
14

I jumped up, but then couldn't think what to do. The actor was still and stiff, his eyes wide and staring and all the color gone from his face. Then he started shaking violently.

"What's the matter, man?" Captain Dale grabbed his shoulder. He jerked his hand back. "He's cold as ice!"

People clustered around the actor. I stood on the bench to see better, balancing against the gentle swaying of the boat. Tania jumped up beside me and grabbed my arm. "The ghost didn't like what he was hearing. He didn't realize it was just a joke, I guess. He thought the actor was really going to wreck the boat."

"So what did he do? Go inside him, take him over, like Rose did with you?"

"No, just kind of grabbed him, like he wanted to shake him." Tania stood on her toes and craned her neck, clutching my arm for balance. "I can't quite see. There's too many people around."

The group shifted, and Mom led the actor over to a deck chair. "Mr. Simpson! Charlie! Please, are you all right?"

He collapsed into a chair. Tania sighed and loosened her grip on my arm. "Mr. O'Brien is moving away now. Maybe it was hearing the man's real name that did it. I'm going to go talk to him." She jumped down and started across the deck.

I hesitated for a minute, wanting to follow her, but not wanting to miss anything here. The actor was blinking and shivering. Maggie grabbed a coat from a chair and wrapped it around his shoulders.

Bruce bounced over, grinning like a maniac. "This is amazing! Do you realize what happened? It had to be the ghost! He heard us talking about him, and he . . . he . . ." He paused a minute, like he wasn't sure what Henry O'Brien had been doing. "He wanted to give us a message, tell us how he felt about all this, or something. Amazing!"

I had forgotten about Madame Natasha, but of course now she strode into the middle of the group. Her voice rang out. "I shall talk to him!" She knelt before the actor, then glanced over to make sure a camera was trained on her and running. "Mr. O'Brien," she said in a low, spooky voice. "Henry O'Brien! Do not possess this poor man. He means you no harm. We only want to help you."

The actor stared at her, then glanced around as if looking for help. Madame Natasha threw her head back and moaned. "Oh, Henry O'Brien, let us help you find peace!"

The actor looked at Bruce. "I . . . I don't think he's here anymore. I mean, that weird cold feeling is gone. But if you want me to pretend—"

I got up. The show wasn't over, but there wasn't anything else I needed to see.

I spotted Tania across the deck and went to her. She was standing by the railing, turned a little sideways. I tried to figure out where she was looking, so I could avoid walking through the ghost again.

She was frowning, listening to something. "Hey, what's up?" I mumbled.

She held up a hand to tell me to wait. She shook her head. "It's not like that. You have to believe me. They're just actors, pretending. Do you know what an actor is? Did you ever go to the theater when . . . when you were in this world?"

I felt someone come up behind me. I whipped around and found myself facing Maggie.

"That was pretty strange," she said.

"Uh . . . um, yeah. It was."

Tania blinked a couple of times. "Oh, yes." Her eyes darted sideways, but she faced us when she spoke. "He was just an actor, of course. I mean, they weren't really going to do anything bad to the boat. But Mr. O'Brien thought they were."

Maggie grinned. "You sound like you're becoming a believer."

"Oh, well, you know, if there was anything to it at all."

"There's something," Maggie said. "That man was freezing cold. Even if he'd had some reason to fake it, I don't see how he could have." She shrugged. "It's all a mystery to me. But I guess it's going to be a while before we get organized again. You two can get out on the landing if you want." She winked at me. "It looks like you could find some ice cream at that Snack Shack."

"Yeah, maybe," I said. I looked toward shore. A few dozen people had gathered there. I figured they were just townspeople, you know, come to watch the shooting. A little town like that probably didn't get a TV show every day. "Wait, who are those people?"

Maggie turned to look. Tania ducked back and I heard her whisper something to the ghost, but I tried to keep Maggie's attention on the dock. "That's no home video camera," I said, pointing at a guy holding a big camera like the ones the TV crew used.

"It sure isn't. What's it say on the side—sixty-two? It must be a local news station. Well!" Maggie glanced over to where Madame Natasha was still pretending to talk to the ghost. "Bruce will be pleased. He's always trying to get publicity for the show, but it's not easy."

"There's a guy making notes on a pad, too." I leaned sideways on the railing and casually glanced back at Tania. She had moved a little farther away and was whispering frantically. If anyone noticed her she'd look completely loony, talking and gesturing to thin air.

"That's the kind newspaper reporters use," Maggie said. "Better and better." She started to turn.

"Hey, Tania!" I hollered. It came out way louder than I meant, and Maggie jumped. I cleared my throat and tried to smile. "Look, reporters! Maybe we'll get on the news!"

Tania's eyes widened and she stepped back until she hit the wall. "No thanks. They didn't—I mean, they couldn't . . . see me just now, could they?"

I grinned at Maggie. "She's camera shy."

Maggie chuckled. "Me too. Let's let Bruce handle them." She strode across the deck toward him.

I slumped back against the railing. "Whew. You'd

better be more careful if you don't want people getting suspicious. You can't just stand here in plain sight talking to nothing."

Tania glanced sideways. "I'm trying to explain things to Mr. O'Brien."

"And, um, what does he think?" I had to remember to watch what I said. He could hear me, even if I couldn't hear him.

"I've told him we want to help him, but he says there's nothing we can do." Tania looked at the blank space and gulped. "All right, except stay away, he says. But Mr. O'Brien, it's not Jon's fault that he has to be up there in the pilothouse. They're making him."

"I won't do any harm," I said. "It's really interesting, learning how to run a boat. I bet I could be good at it."

"Wait!" Tania shrieked. She stumbled forward, arms reaching out. I leapt toward her to catch her.

Too late, I realized she wasn't talking to me or reaching for me. Her hand moved like she was grabbing an invisible arm. She gasped and pulled back, hugging her hand to her body.

My momentum carried me forward, even as I tried to stop. I felt the cold first on my arms, like icy vise grips squeezing my biceps. Then waves of cold flowed down to my hands, up to my shoulders, all through my body.

I tried to breathe, but my chest felt too tight.

My vision blurred, darkened. The last thing I saw was Tania's horrified face.

And I fell.

CHAPTER
15

Cold. Dark. Like floating through space.

A dim light, beyond my eyelids. The hard floor, pressing into my shoulder and head. Murmuring voices.

Voices?

I opened my eyes and blinked against the bright sun. Figures wavered in my vision.

I struggled to sit up, but hands held me down. A face pushed close to mine, blocking the sunlight. "Jon? Jon, baby, are you all right?"

I closed my eyes again, hoping it would all go away.

"Jon! Honey, speak to me!"

I sighed and opened my eyes. "Hi, Mom. I'm okay."

"What happened? Call a doctor! Somebody, an ambulance—"

"No!" I sat up, pushing her hands away, and tried to

act like the world wasn't spinning. "I don't need a doctor. I'm fine."

"But you fainted! Last month, Tania, and now you! What's going wrong with my children?"

My vision had cleared, but I kind of wished it hadn't. It was like everybody in the world was looking down at me. Bruce, the captain, Madame Natasha, and . . .

I dragged my gaze away from Maggie and looked for Tania. She was squatting next to me. "I didn't faint," I said, begging her for help with my eyes. "I just . . . just . . ."

"He tripped," Tania said. "He just stumbled and fell."

"A concussion!" Mom cried.

"I didn't hit my head or anything. Just got a bit confused for second. I'm fine now."

Maggie crouched and looked into my face. "You're awfully pale. And sweating." How humiliating.

"Too much sun?" Bruce asked.

"Yes!" I said. "That's it, it's what-do-you-call it, heatstroke. Just a little too much sun. A glass of water and I'll be fine."

Mom was rubbing my arms. "But you're so cold! Almost like . . ." She turned and looked vaguely toward the open deck. I knew she was remembering the actor's chill.

"That's one of the symptoms of heatstroke." I tried to sound confident. "I remember it from Scouts. You can get a chill. It's, like, backward from what you'd think."

Maggie put a hand on my forehead. My heart jumped a couple of times.

"Actually, you get hot and dry with heatstroke, but victims of heat exhaustion can be cool, pale, and sweaty. Also dizzy. Fortunately, heat exhaustion isn't as serious as heatstroke."

"Yeah, that's it," I croaked. "I knew it was something like that. Nothing to worry about." I wished all those people would go away. Well, except maybe Maggie. I couldn't quite decide if having her worried about me was more nice or embarrassing.

"But shouldn't we get him to a doctor, to be sure?" Mom said.

I took her hands and looked into her face. "Mom, please. There are all kinds of reporters out there on that dock. Please don't make this some big public spectacle." *Even more than it already is,* I added in my mind. "I promise I'll take it easy, stay in the shade, drink lots of water. Anything you say—just don't make a fuss in front of the news camera."

Bruce whipped around and leaned over the railing. "News camera? He's right!"

Mom glanced at him, then looked back at me.

Bruce pushed through the crowd of *Haunted* staff and boat crewmen. "They're trying to get on board," Bruce said. "Come on, Annette. Publicity!"

The crowd started to drift off, lured by a better show. Mom kept clutching my hands, looking worried.

Maggie put a hand on her shoulder. "Go ahead, Annette. I'll look after these kids. Bruce needs you. The show must go on, right?"

Mom looked from her, to me, to Tania, and finally back at Maggie. "You'll take good care of them?"

"You bet."

Finally, after a hug and a big kiss on the cheek—very embarrassing—Mom went to join the others.

None of us said anything for a minute. Finally, Maggie sighed. "I don't suppose there's any chance you'll tell me what really happened?"

I wanted to tell her. At least, I wanted to tell her *something*—something that wouldn't make me look like a weakling or an idiot. First Mick called me a vandal, and then I collapsed in front of everybody. Talk about failing to make a good impression.

Tania and I exchanged a glance. I was finding it hard to look at Maggie. And I couldn't think of a single thing to say.

Maggie sighed again. "No, I didn't think so. Well, is there anything I can do?"

My throat felt tight. I couldn't meet her eyes. Tania just shook her head and whispered, "Thank you."

Maggie nodded. "Hey, here's a fun fact from my research. The Mississippi is muddy, and the Missouri is even worse. If a man jumps into the Missouri River, they say, he's more likely to break a leg than to drown. People used to drink the river water, of course. But they said you could only drink from the Mississippi if you had some other water to wash it down with."

I gave her a weak smile without really looking at her. It just made me feel worse that she was trying to cheer us up.

"Oh, boy." Something in Maggie's voice had changed, and I risked a glance at her. She was looking toward the crowd on deck and starting to smile. "Well, if you're feeling up to it now, you might want to watch this show."

Somehow in the shuffle, Madame Natasha had reached the reporters first. Fortunately, we were close enough to hear, though off to the side of the cameras.

"Thank you for coming," Madame Natasha said, her red hair shining like a bonfire. "As promised, we have a fascinating tale to tell."

"That sneak," Maggie muttered. "She must have called the press herself."

"It is not always easy being psychic," Madame N

said. "Though many envy us our gifts in reaching to other worlds, the work is challenging . . . even dangerous." She said the last word in a kind of spooky voice. "Take the case I'm working on now. The ghost of poor Henry O'Brien, the steamship pilot who caused a disaster."

"Steam*boat*," I muttered.

A few of the townspeople made jeering comments, but Madame N just spoke a little louder as she quickly summarized the ghost story.

"They should let the captain tell it," Tania said. "He does it lots better."

"Looks like Bruce doesn't know what to do with himself," I said. He was hovering nearby, like he wanted to break in but couldn't figure out how.

A woman reporter moved next to Madame Natasha. "Are you claiming that you actually saw the ghost yourself?"

Madame N gave a slow nod. "Indeed. This very afternoon. He took over the body of a man on the boat, an actor playing the ghost's part in a reenactment."

The actor pushed forward, grabbing his chance in the spotlight, and described the experience.

Tania snorted. "If she could actually see the ghost, why didn't she warn anyone *before* he took over the actor?"

"Bruce better get in there or he'll lose his chance,"

Maggie said. "They'll probably cut this whole thing down to fifteen seconds for the evening news."

Madame Natasha cut off the actor to tell how she had "rescued" him. Then she held up a book. "You can read many dramatic stories like this in my new book, *Triumphs and Tragedies of a Psychic Sleuth*."

"Oh, please," Maggie groaned.

Bruce finally pushed his way in front of the camera. He put an arm around Madame N. "And we here at *Haunted* TV are proud to announce our new partnership with Madame Natasha. Look for her as a guest on many of our upcoming shows! See us at ten p.m. on—"

"Well, that's interesting," Maggie said. "I wonder when he came up with that plan." She shook her head. "I hope it doesn't come back to bite him. Looks like we'll be stuck with that annoying woman for some time."

The reporters packed up and left. The *Haunted* crew came back on board. Madame Natasha drifted off, looking pleased with herself. Bruce tried to put his arm around Mom, but she shrugged him off. "But angel," he said, "it's a great opportunity for the show. I couldn't pass it up! You know what our ratings are like. . . ."

Mom mumbled something I couldn't hear, then turned away from him and stormed over to us. She spoke in a low voice, emphasizing each word. "I cannot stand that woman!"

Tania and I took the chance to slip away as Maggie commiserated with Mom.

"I wish we could do something about the fraud," Tania said. "She makes Mom unhappy and she's poking in our business. We've just got to get rid of her."

I rubbed my hands over my face and yawned. I still felt kind of weak after my ghost encounter. "One thing at a time, okay? Let's deal with Henry O'Brien first."

Tania got that look in her eyes. The one that means trouble ahead. My stomach went cold, and I knew this time it wasn't from any ghost.

"But maybe they're not separate problems," Tania said. "Mr. O'Brien seems ready to believe the worst of everybody. And if there's one person who deserves it, it's Madame Natasha!"

"You want to sic Henry O'Brien on her?"

"Why not? It's about time a ghost did us a favor."

CHAPTER
16

I stopped and turned to face her. I couldn't think and walk at the same time, not when I had that much to think about. "Look, first of all, I'm already in trouble. And second, just how do you expect to get the ghost to go after Madame Natasha?"

She frowned, looking fierce, and paced in tight circles while she talked. "All right, Madame Natasha seems to have figured out that I can see ghosts. And now she wants to be my best buddy. So I can go to her and tell her that the ghost told me something. That there's something wrong with the boat, and she has to fix it. Then I'll find the ghost and tell him that Madame Natasha is wrecking things."

I thought for a minute, looking for flaws. Hoping I'd find enough to discourage her. "We already tried the fake sabotage, and it didn't work. I doubt you could get Madame N to loosen bolts, and I'm sure not going to do it to pretend that's the problem."

Tania wrinkled her nose and thought for a minute. "Maybe I can tell her that the ghost is in the boiler room, and she should go there to talk to him. She'll get in trouble just going in there."

"They'll just turn her back at the door. There's always someone on duty in there, I think."

"I'll tell her there's something wrong, and she needs to go fix it. She'll make a fool of herself trying to get in, and they won't find anything wrong."

"Well, okay, but—"

"And while she's on her way, I'll find Henry O'Brien and tell him he has to stop her."

"Tania," I moaned, "is this really necessary? I thought you wanted to help the ghost."

Her eyes widened. "But I am! Mr. O'Brien will trust me more after this. And getting rid of Madame Natasha means she won't be able to interfere."

"Okay, fine, do whatever you want. But I'm supposed to get back up to the pilothouse and work."

"Everybody knows you just passed out." I winced at the reminder. "You're supposed to have heat exhaustion, right?" Tania said. "No one will expect you to get right back to work."

"So I suppose you want me to . . . What exactly do you want me to do?"

"Just help me find Madame Natasha. I'd better do all the talking. You're a terrible liar."

"Thanks. Look, you'd better figure out where the ghost is first. You won't have time to go running all over the boat once you get Flamehead going."

"He's probably up at the pilothouse. I'll check."

"I'll wait here," I muttered as she bounced off. I leaned against the wall and closed my eyes. Being grabbed by a ghost took a lot out of you. Having a nutty little sister did, too.

I'd been resting for a minute or so when I felt a presence—like someone was watching me. My heart raced as I straightened and opened my eyes.

Madame Natasha smiled at me—if you can call any expression that creepy a smile. "Jon, you poor boy, how are you feeling? I just wanted to see if you were all right after your . . . little spell."

"Uh, yeah, fine," I mumbled.

She stepped closer—too close—and looked into my face. "Tell me, how did you feel just before you fainted? Did you see or hear anything unusual?"

My eyes darted left and right, like I couldn't even control them. Madame Natasha might be a sneak and a liar, but she wasn't dumb. She wouldn't be interested in me if she didn't think my "spell" had something to do with the ghost.

I took a deep breath and forced myself to look into her face. I even smiled. "I'm not real observant. But you know, Tania was just looking for you. I think she had something she wanted to tell you."

Her face lit up with excitement—or maybe triumph. "Where is she?"

Fortunately, before I had to answer, I heard quick, light footsteps and then Tania rounded the corner. I tried to give her a meaningful look. "I just told Madame Natasha you're looking for her."

Tania turned on the innocent charm. "Oh, yes," she gushed as she hurried forward. "I'm so glad I found you!" She paused and gave a coy, shy look. "I guess you figured out that, well . . ." She looked around to make sure we were alone, then whispered, "I can see ghosts."

Madame Natasha gushed right back at her. "Oh, my dear, I'm so glad you decided to trust me! I can be a great help to you."

"I know." Tania nodded. "But you see, I don't want anybody to know. I'll explain that later. But the important thing is, Henry O'Brien told me that there's a problem with the boat, in the boiler room. Someone needs to go fix it. But I can't tell anyone, because I don't want them to know he talked to me." She looked up with her big blue eyes wide, the picture of helpless innocence. "So could you take care of it?"

Madame Natasha's eyes shone. "What exactly did the ghost tell you?"

Tania bit her lip. "He says there's a, um, a valve thing, that's not working."

"Which valve? Where?"

Tania gave me a helpless glance. "I'm not very good with mechanical things." I realized that she'd only glanced in the boiler room, and hadn't thought to ask me about it.

I shrugged. "Don't look at me. I didn't hear anything the ghost said."

Tania shot me a microsecond glare, then went on. "Okay. He said it was the main valve that controls the steam. Something's wrong with it, and you need to turn it off."

That sounded pretty reasonable, on a steamboat. Madame Natasha smiled. "You're a good girl. Don't worry, I'll take care of everything. Come on, we'd better hurry."

"Oh, not me," Tania said. "I don't want to be involved."

"But my dear, I need you . . ." You could practically see the war going on inside her. She didn't want to admit that she couldn't see the ghost herself. Finally, she said, "You can help me with the ghost. He may decide he'd rather speak to you. Sometimes ghosts prefer to talk to children."

Tania scrunched up her face. "Oh, all right. But you go ahead and I'll stay out of sight unless you need me."

Madame Natasha hesitated, but Tania added, "You'd better hurry. The boat could explode or something if you don't get to it in time!"

Madame Natasha strode off. Tania rolled her eyes. "What a sneak." I didn't bother to point out who'd been doing the lying this time. "I'll go get Henry O'Brien," she said. "You keep an eye on *her*."

Since that task didn't seem likely to get me in trouble—and might provide a good show—I followed Madame N. She peered at her reflection in a window and played with her hair. Then she walked right past the boiler room. I almost called out to her, but remembered in time that there wasn't really an emergency. Let her take her time.

I trailed behind her as she went out on the main deck. Bruce had his arm around Mom and was saying something to her. She was smiling—until she saw Madame N.

The fraud spoke only to Bruce. "You must come at once! The ghost has told me of a danger in the boiler room. He has asked me to fix it. Bring the cameras."

I groaned. We should have expected this, with the pseudo-psychic's obsession with publicity. I wondered how having everyone on the boat witness this setup would affect Tania's plan. Maybe it was better. A public humiliation would be worse than just getting a chill.

Or maybe Madame Natasha would blame the whole thing on Tania and me.

Bruce was bounding around like crazy man, calling to the camera operators. Mom scowled at him. Then she and Maggie exchanged glances, shook their heads, and smiled. I'm not sure what all that meant.

Finally, the whole crew trailed after Madame Natasha. Bruce and the first cameraman were in the lead. I shrugged and joined the crowd. Whatever happened next, it was going to happen in front of everyone.

CHAPTER

Madame Natasha stopped at the boiler room door.
I stayed back and craned my neck to see over
the crowd. She gave the cameraman a minute to
get in place, then pushed the door open.

As she stepped through, Cleavon leaped forward.
He blocked her and forced her to back out. "Sorry, lady,
no passengers allowed in here." He stopped and gaped
at the crowd. "What the hey?"

Madame Natasha turned a three-quarters profile to
the camera and put on her regal airs. "We are in danger!
There is a problem with one of your valves, and I have
come to help."

Cleavon shook his head. "There ain't nothing wrong.
Me and Miguel been on duty all day, and we know what
we're doing. And you can't come in here, 'less the captain says so."

Madame Natasha drew herself up so she could look

down at Cleavon. He was shorter than she was, but probably fifty pounds heavier with solid muscle. "A captain has said so!" Madame N insisted. "Captain Henry O'Brien, who still watches over this boat."

Cleavon threw back his head and laughed. He wiped his eyes and said, "That's a good one. Sorry, lady, but Henry O'Brien ain't been on duty for almost a century now. Anyway, he weren't no captain, just a pilot."

Tania appeared at my side. "Oh, good grief. She would cause a circus."

"Of course. Did you—"

Tania had turned to talk to the empty space at her other side. "You see what she's doing? She's trying to get into the boiler room. You have to stop her."

She listened a moment, then stamped her foot. "But what if she gets past him? I really think *you* ought to do something. I'm telling you, that woman is trouble!"

She turned as if watching him walk away. I could tell Henry O'Brien moved through the crowd, even if I couldn't actually see him. People kind of jumped and turned to look over their shoulders, then rubbed themselves like they had a chill. They started prodding each other and whispering.

Cleavon was saying, "Tell you what, I'll go double-check all the valves and things. You'll just have to trust me to take care of it." He backed into the boiler room and closed the door.

Madame Natasha frowned at it a moment, then turned toward the camera with a smile. "So you see, disaster averted! Because the ghost came to me with a warning, the ship is safe."

The cameraman's head popped up. "Hey, we're getting fogged up again."

Madame Natasha shivered, then her face lit up. "Henry O'Brien!" she exclaimed, just as if she could see him in front of her. "Never fear, I have acted on your warning."

"What's O'Brien doing?" I whispered to Tania.

She sighed. "Asking her questions."

"Together, we have saved the ship!" Madame Natasha went on. "On behalf of all the passengers and crew, I thank you."

"Now he's getting confused, because she seems to be talking to him but not listening to him." Tania bounced up and down. "Oh, good, he's reaching out for her!"

Madame Natasha shuddered and swayed. But she was pretty tough. She grabbed the door frame with a hand and took a couple of deep breaths. "You can go now," she gasped, "back to . . . back to your place. . . . All is well!"

"Darn it, he's leaving." Tania folded her arms and slumped back against the wall.

Madame Natasha straightened and started to get some color back. She made a few last comments to the camera, which I couldn't hear because everyone was whispering.

The crowd started to move off. Bruce was beside Madame Natasha, saying, "That was amazing. Just wonderful! You have such a gift."

As they went past us, Madame Natasha stepped aside and leaned close to Tania. "Thank you, my dear," she whispered. "I won't forget your help."

She turned away again before she could see Tania's sour expression. Then we were alone. I opened my mouth, but after one glance at Tania's face, I shut it again. Anything I could say at that point would just get me kicked.

Finally, Tania smiled, but not at me, and I realized we weren't alone after all. "You see, you stopped her from causing an accident." After a pause, she added, "Well, no, I don't understand her either. But trust me, she's a troublemaker." Another pause. "All right, bye."

I watched her watch him walk away. She kicked her heel against the wall. "Well, that was a bust."

"Yeah." I couldn't think of anything else to say. Finally, I shrugged. "Guess I'll go back up to the pilot-house."

Tania sighed. "Yeah. That's just what Henry O'Brien said."

❖

I was still thinking about Madame Natasha when I opened the pilothouse door. Maybe that's why my mind went blank when I saw Maggie. She was standing with her hands on the wheel, as if she were steering. Bruce was taking a picture of her with a cell phone camera.

He passed it back, and she laughed as she looked at the picture. "That's great. David will get a kick out of it. You know, we go on these trips surrounded by movie cameras, and I never have a picture of myself." She glanced up. "Hi, Jon."

"Hey." I wanted to ask who David was, but couldn't get up the nerve.

"Jon, hey!" Bruce crossed the small room and slapped me on the shoulder. "The captain tells me you've been working hard today. Good boy."

"Um." I felt a little like a dog that had been patted on the head. I don't always know how to act around Bruce. I think he feels the same way about me. As stepfathers go, he could be a lot worse, I guess. It's just weird to be suddenly related to someone you hardly know.

"Your turn at the wheel?" Maggie asked. I glanced at the captain, then back at her. She was joking, right? She didn't really think they'd put me in charge of the boat. But if she did, I didn't want to tell her otherwise.

"Come on, photo op," she said, gesturing at the wheel.

Oh. Just for a picture. I moved to the wheel and grinned.

"Great. Now look out the window like you're really steering." I felt my face go hot, but tried to look serious, like I was studying the river ahead. She snapped a couple more photos, and then Mr. Hendrickson took the wheel again. I remembered what Cleavon said about Henry O'Brien being a pilot rather than a captain. I guess the pilot was in charge of steering the boat, and the captain was in charge of everything.

"Should be just a couple of more minutes," Mr. Hendrickson said.

"We're going by the place where the accident happened," Maggie said.

"You're going to film it?" I asked.

Maggie shrugged. Bruce said, "We'll check it out first. There may not be anything worth filming. But maybe just a few seconds of the river, with a voice-over."

"The river's changed a lot since those days," Captain Dale said. "This is one spot where it actually flows in the same channel. Years ago, the Army Corps of Engineers straightened the river, getting rid of horseshoe bends. Then they shored up the banks so the river doesn't change course anymore. They've done a lot to tame the river—though she sometimes has a few surprises for them when it storms."

I looked out the window. The river ran straight ahead, wide enough that you couldn't throw a stone and hit either side. Thick trees lined the bank. The sun glittered on the water. It was hard to imagine anything surprising. I pictured the Loch Ness Monster rising up out of the water, and chuckled.

"Here we go," Mr. Hendrickson said. He gestured to the left bank. "According to the records, it was right up there. They cleared the snag out long ago, of course."

Maggie, Bruce, and I went out onto the deck. "So that's where it happened," Maggie said. Her eyes narrowed as she gazed at the shore. "People screaming, panicking. Dying." She shook her head. "It looks so peaceful now."

"Nothing much worth filming." Bruce turned back toward the pilothouse.

A cold breeze washed across the deck. Goose bumps rose on my arms.

Maggie hugged herself and shivered. "Wow, must be a cold front coming in."

I looked around. Not a cloud in the sky.

The wind picked up and swirled around. Dust and a few leaves rose from the deck in a spiral, like a miniature tornado. My nose and ears started to tingle with cold. This was no ordinary storm.

CHAPTER
18

It had to be the ghost. Upset to see the accident site? Angry that we brought him here? I wished Tania was here to tell me what she saw and heard. At the same time, I was glad she was safe below.

The engines thrummed, and the deck vibrated underfoot. Over it all, the wind howled. Maggie grabbed the railing and shouted above the wind. "We'd better get inside."

I wanted to take her arm, to help her. But she pushed away from the railing, head bent against the wind. She crossed her arms over her chest, hugging herself against the cold.

I tried to follow. A blast of icy wind knocked me back. I hooked an arm over the railing as I stumbled. It felt like the wind wanted to push me off the boat. Maggie glanced back. "Keep going!" I shouted as I struggled to my feet. No way did I want her rescuing me.

I hunched over and pushed into the howling wind. I had to fight for each step. My face felt numb, and my teeth ached with the cold. The wind roared in my ears. I thought I heard screaming, shrieks of fear and pain, swirling around me.

Then I swear I smelled smoke—something burning. I whipped my head around. A dark cloud seemed to rush around the deck, though the sky above shone blue. I remembered the name *hurricane deck*. I had to get inside.

I reached the front of the pilothouse and used the window frames to pull myself along the wall. I kept my head down against the bitter wind and flying dust. Finally, I rounded the corner. From inside, Maggie threw her weight against the door to push it open. I squeezed through the gap and staggered in.

The door slammed shut behind me. I swayed, adjusting to the lack of wind. Mr. Hendrickson was hauling on the wheel. Captain Dale checked the instruments. They shouted to each other over the noise of wind and creaking wood.

The pilothouse shook with the force of the winds. I half expected it to pick up and fly away, like the house in *The Wizard of Oz*.

"This is ridiculous!" Maggie shouted. "I've never seen anything like it!"

Bruce's perfect hair was blown every which way. His eyes shone with delight. "It's the ghost! It has to be. He's reacting to the accident site."

I looked out the window. On the shore, trees whipped back and forth, leaves scattering in the air. The shoreline seemed to be moving as we went sideways to the river. The boat was turning. I hoped Mr. Hendrickson was doing it on purpose.

He and the captain were leaning on the wheel, pulling it over to the right. I joined them. "Can I help?"

Captain Dale nodded. "Put your weight into it!" I took the other side of the wheel and pushed up. The boat shuddered and screeched. I wasn't sure how much was from the wind, and how much from the sharp turn.

Bruce yelled over the noise. "We've got to get the cameras! Let's get this on film."

The boat finished the turn and was pointing downstream. Mr. Hendrickson and the captain straightened. "All right, lad, that's enough," Captain Dale said.

I stepped back, gasping, as Mr. Hendrickson took the wheel alone. The captain moved to the lever that told the engineers to go faster. Bells rang, and the dial moved to show that they'd followed the command. We moved quickly away from the accident site. The shuddering and screeching stopped.

"The wind's dying down," Maggie said. She spoke

in a normal voice, and we could hear her, though the wind's roar still echoed in my ears.

"No, wait!" Bruce said. "We have to get this on film."

Captain Dale shook his head. "We're getting out of here. We're not risking the whole boat."

Bruce protested, and Maggie calmed him down. I looked at the captain. "Do you believe that was the ghost?"

He shook his head. "I don't know what to believe. When I'm on land, it's easy to say ghosts don't exist. But I know better than to argue with the river. We don't usually bring the *Delta Belle* this way. After what just happened, I don't think I'll start."

Mom burst through the pilothouse door. "What was that? What happened?"

Bruce explained. I sank down on a bench against the wall. I still felt stiff with cold. I flexed my fingers and they tingled as the blood returned.

Mom crossed to me. "Jon, honey, are you all right?" Before I could answer, she was fussing with my hair. "Just look at you! You're pale and chilled." She laid a hand on my cheek.

"I'm all right," I said, trying to shrug her away.

"I want you to go right down to your room and lie down. Bundle up in bed and get warm."

"Mom," I groaned. I glanced at Maggie. She was turned away, looking out the window, but she had to hear us.

"Don't bother arguing," Mom said. "You've had a hard day, first fainting and now this. You're going to go down and take a nap."

I closed my eyes and sighed. "Fine." I know when I'm beat. Arguing would just increase my humiliation. But I managed to get away without a hug or a kiss.

I didn't think I'd be able to sleep, but I did. I had weird dreams, though. I kept feeling like someone was calling me, and I had to get up and warn everyone about a problem with the boat, but I couldn't wake up. I don't think that was the ghost's influence. I mean, not directly. I think it was just all the stuff that was in my head.

By the time I woke up properly and got out again, they'd set the tables for dinner. We had buffalo burgers, and the captain talked about how they used to send out hunting parties from the steamboat on long journeys. Sometimes the hunter would get a buffalo or deer, and sometimes Indians would get a hunter!

"Of course, this is just a little boat," Captain Dale said. "Now you take the *Hurronico*. She was so big, her hull was jointed so she could get around the bends."

I tried to picture a steamboat with a joint in the

middle, like some city buses. I couldn't quite figure out how it would work.

"Then there's the *E. Jenkins*," Captain Dale said. "She was so big it took a whole season for her wheel to go around once. Or the *Jim Johnson*, famous for her tall smokestacks. They put out the fires each fall, and smoke would still be coming out in the spring."

I chuckled, and tried to pretend that I had known from the start that he was joking.

Bruce was happy at dinner—talking a lot and smiling this big goofy grin. I guess Mom was happy because he was happy. Madame Natasha looked proud. She kept shooting Tania these sly little grins, the kind that say, "We share a secret." So of course, Tania was fuming.

I gave her a nudge and kept my voice low. "Relax. You'll have other chances to get her. Looks like she'll be with the show for a long time."

"Great. But she's not even the worst of it. Bruce has all the footage he needs, so we're turning back early and leaving the boat tomorrow. I need more time! Maybe if I could steal or ruin some of his film, he'd have to stay—"

"Don't even go there. What's gotten into you?"

"I have to help Henry O'Brien! I couldn't even talk to him this afternoon, with him up in the pilothouse and other people around. And of course you were in bed."

"Hey, not my fault. Complain to Mom. Anyway, why is this such a big deal? I know you felt sorry for Rose, because she was crazy sad and missed her husband. So you helped her move on. Good for you. But you don't have to save every ghost that comes along. What's the big deal if Henry O'Brien stays on the boat? He seems to like it here well enough."

"Oh, you just don't get it!" Tania slumped back in her chair and scowled. Then she sat up and leaned toward me. "Look, how would you like to be a ghost, stuck here for eternity?"

"I don't know, it might be cool—kind of like living forever."

"But you can't do whatever you want. You're stuck in one memory, one time. You're reliving the worst moment of your entire life."

CHAPTER
19

Wow. I thought about worst moments. I'd had plenty of bad ones—getting teased or bullied. Having chickenpox or the flu. It had been bad when Mom and Dad told us they were getting divorced. It had been bad before that, with all the fights and tears.

But the worst moment was easy. That was when Angela died. It was bad in so many ways. Awful seeing Mom broken up, so red-faced and puffy from crying that she didn't even look like my mother. Awful seeing Dad go white and still, pulling back from everyone. Awful hearing Tania shriek as she refused to let go of Angela's hand, refused to believe our sister was dead.

And worst of all, that sick, empty feeling as I looked at the little girl I had hugged and cuddled and played with. The child who was gone forever. Having to give up the hope that she might get better—the stupid, crazy hope we held on to, even after the doctors told us the treatments were failing.

That's not a moment I would want to relive, ever. Certainly not over and over for a hundred years. Or for eternity.

Angela hadn't become a ghost. At least, Tania had never seen any sign of her. But what if she had been trapped? I'd want someone to help her move on.

That made me feel more sorry for Henry O'Brien. And for what Tania was trying to do.

People like to say that everything happens for a reason. I heard that a lot when Angela got cancer and when she died. I hated it. There's no reason good enough for a five-year-old to die. If Tania's gift came out of that— if that was the trade—it wasn't good enough. It wasn't fair.

But maybe Angela had to die anyway. And that gave Tania this need to help others who had died. That was something. Some little good that came out of something rotten.

"Jon? Jon, baby, are you all right?"

"What?" I realized I'd spaced out. "Yeah, I'm fine."

Mom put her hand to my forehead. I tried to squirm away, but it's hard when you're trapped in a chair. "You're pale," she said.

"That's because you made me stay inside all afternoon instead of getting out in the sun." I was trying to make it a joke, but it came out whiny.

"You'd better go right back to bed—"

"Mom! I've been in bed for hours. I couldn't sleep if you paid me. I'm fine!"

"I'm just worried about you."

"Well, don't be." It sounded rude, but I couldn't help it. I tried to sink into my chair, out of sight.

Of all people, Bruce stuck up for me. He patted Mom's arm. "Let him be. Fussing won't help."

Everyone was watching me. Madame Natasha looked down her nose. The captain's eyes twinkled. Maggie looked like she was trying not to laugh.

I had to do something to show I wasn't just a little kid with an overprotective mommy. "Captain," I said, "does the boat run all night?"

"Absolutely. We'll go all night and should dock before noon."

"Well, I didn't get to work much this afternoon. I've hardly done anything. So would it be all right if I went up for the night shift?"

Mom made this upset sound, but Captain Dale nodded slowly. "That could be a big help. We usually keep two people on duty at all times, but the second pilot on the night shift had the discourtesy to get food poisoning just before we left. If you'll stay up there for a few hours, the rest of us can get some sleep and then share the shifts for the rest of the night."

I could feel myself grinning. The captain actually trusted me to take a real shift!

"But that's ridiculous," Mom said. "He's just a child. You can't possibly give him that kind of responsibility."

Thanks, Mom.

Captain Dale just smiled. "Don't worry, he won't be steering the boat. The pilot on night shift, Mr. West, has years of experience. It's just federal law that we always have two people available at night. The second doesn't have to be a pilot, just somebody present and awake."

Mom tried to argue, but the captain and Bruce overruled her. We finally agreed that I'd be relieved at midnight, and if I got too tired before then I could wake someone early.

We got up from dinner. As I started for the door, I felt a light touch on my arm. I turned and found myself looking into Maggie's eyes. My heart jumped into my throat.

"I'm sure you're going to do great tonight, Jon."

I swallowed a couple of times but couldn't get any words out. She smiled and moved past me.

I'd been trying to escape before Mom could offer more advice. But after Maggie's comment, I kind of forgot how to walk. Mom caught up, blocking the door and stopping traffic. "You be sure to ask for help if you need it. If you get tired—"

I just nodded and let her ramble. Finally, Bruce interrupted. "Come on, Annette. It's not like he'll be alone."

"Maybe I should go up there myself, keep him company—"

"No. He'll be fine. He'll have someone watching him the whole time."

The discussion might have gone on all night, but Maggie stuck her head back in and interrupted. "We'd better get the cameras set up if we're going to use that nice dusk light for the disaster scene."

"Oh. Oh, right." Mom gave me one last worried look, grabbed me, and kissed my cheek. Then she hurried off with Bruce. I'm glad there's something that can distract her from her intensive mothering. I guess she's kind of like a mother to the whole crew, so that lets her get some of it out of her system.

The camera operators got their cameras. The makeup artist touched up the actor playing Henry O'Brien. Everyone crowded onto the upper deck. Tania and I slipped in while Mick was distracted by badgering someone else.

They put one camera in the open doorway, looking into the pilothouse. Another stood farther out. That one had a shot that showed the pilothouse, the front of the boat, and the river beyond. We all had to stay behind the cameras. In the film, you wouldn't know anyone was there, besides the lead actor. We were in a wide spot on the river, and they'd slowed the engines so the boat hardly moved. Still, Captain Dale and Mr. Hendrickson hovered nearby, keeping an eye on things.

Even though the disaster would really have happened late at night, they wanted to shoot at dusk. That way the cameras had enough light to see some of the surrounding river. A few small lights set up in the pilothouse illuminated "Henry O'Brien," but the room would still look dark on camera.

Bruce turned to Tania and me, where we leaned against the rail with Maggie. "When I give the signal, I want you all to scream. Tania, give it your best. Remember, this is supposed to be a whole boat full of passengers, with women and children. We can fill in some sound effects in the studio if we have to, but I'd rather get it now."

As he turned away, Tania wrinkled her nose and hunched her shoulders. "I don't know if I can scream on cue."

"Sure you can," Maggie said. "Don't worry about the camera. It won't see you, and nobody will know it's you.

Just watch the shooting and try to get into the spirit of things."

"Well, all right. If you will, too."

Maggie grinned. "I'll scream my head off. It isn't often you get to let out a really good shriek." She leaned closer and whispered, "Just think of screaming at Madame Natasha. That should inspire you."

Tania laughed, and I smiled at Maggie. I wasn't about to scream like a girl—not with Maggie right there. But maybe I could yell something. "Help!" or "Oh no!" or "Look out!" That wouldn't be so bad, especially with everyone else yelling, too.

"Speaking of that endearing lady," Maggie said, "I'd better go over there. If she tries to steal this scene, I'm going to haul her back. Or maybe just pitch her over the side." She squeezed through the crowd and took up a place next to Madame Natasha.

"Places, everyone," Mom called. "Let's see if we can do this in one take." Already the shoreline was blurring and the water was going gray.

The actor hesitated in the doorway. "What happens if . . . well, like earlier. What if it happens again?"

Everyone glanced around. You could see them wondering if the ghost was here. I looked at Tania. She gave a little smile and the slightest hint of a nod. Yeah, this could be interesting.

133

"Just do your best," Bruce said. He turned and whispered to Mom. "Do you think it will happen? We could use that."

Finally, Mom called for quiet on the set, and then action. The actor held on to the wheel. He yawned and rubbed his eyes. He was pretty good—he looked like a tired man trying not to fall asleep. He put his forearm across the wheel and rested his head on it.

I looked down at Tania. She stretched up and put her mouth to my ear. She breathed the words so softly even Mean Mick didn't hear. "It's okay. With all these people around, I guess he's not worried about one sleepy pilot."

After a few more seconds of fake snoozing, the actor threw himself forward against the wheel, and then stumbled back. It really looked like he'd hit something and gotten a jolt. I grabbed the rail behind me, half expecting to feel the crash myself.

The actor looked around, wide-eyed and panicky now. He grabbed the wheel and leaned forward to look over it. "What have I done? We've hit a snag!"

He grabbed for the bell pull. The whistle shattered the quiet night.

Bruce turned and gestured to us. People started shouting and screaming. I joined in, hardly knowing what I was saying.

Tania shrieked. My eardrums sang, until she broke off in the middle. She grabbed my arm. "Jon!" she gasped. "That's done it, now Henry O'Brien is worked up."

"Is he going after the actor?"

"No, he's coming toward us!"

I shoved Tania behind me. People in the crowd gasped and stumbled as the ghost pushed through them. Tania must have been right about his cold getting worse when he was upset.

I felt the icy grip on my arm. "No, leave us alone!" I tried to stay upright, stay conscious. My legs buckled and I slumped sideways against the rail. The grip left my arm, but I could still feel waves of cold radiating from the space next to me.

"It's all right," Tania babbled, "you don't need to help me. There's nothing wrong really, it's just pretend—"

She broke off with a gasp. Her eyes went wide, then rolled back in her head. She moaned and collapsed against the rail, shivering violently.

She snapped straight, her eyes blank and staring. Then she turned. She moved slowly, clumsily, like she'd forgotten how to use her body.

She started to climb over the railing.

CHAPTER

20

What on earth was she doing? I stared, feeling the waves of cold flowing from her.

Then it hit me. Tania wasn't doing anything. It was the ghost. Henry O'Brien had taken over her body.

She put one leg over the railing. It was a straight drop to the cold water below. Henry O'Brien—and Tania—were about to jump overboard.

"No!" I grabbed for her, wrapping my arms around her waist. The cold choked me, froze my lungs and my brain. My arms went numb, so I could hardly control them. But I held on, to Tania and to consciousness, with everything I had.

My eyes stung with frozen tears. My legs trembled. I couldn't take a breath against the crushing cold.

I heard shouts around me. Hands grabbed my arms. I could barely feel them through the numb ache, but I focused on those touches. Concentrated on those tiny bits of less cold.

I stumbled back into the waiting arms. My legs gave out and I collapsed on the deck with Tania sprawled across me. I lay with my eyes closed, gasping for breath. My arms stayed locked around Tania's waist.

Slowly, the warmth came back. Tania moaned and stirred. I had to loosen my fingers one by one. Voices swirled around me, but I didn't bother to sort out the words.

Finally, I opened my eyes. Three feet away, a camera stared into my face, its red light showing the film was running.

Mom knelt beside me and leaned in, blocking that view. "Are you all right?" Her hands fluttered over me and Tania, as if she couldn't figure out who to check first.

"Yeah," I said. "Tania?"

She rolled off me and sat up, hugging her knees. "I'm okay," she whispered. She leaned into Mom, shivering.

The voices kept swirling around us. "Did you see that?" "What happened?"

Of course, Mean Mick had the answer. "He was trying to throw her overboard!" He actually got it right, I thought, until he added, "His own sister, he was throwing her over the railing. Can you believe it?"

I groaned and put my hands over my face. I didn't even have the energy to argue.

I felt Tania stir beside me. When I looked up, she was standing, hands on hips, fire in her eyes. The girl recovers quickly. Maybe it was all that practice she got with the last ghost.

"You idiot! Jon wasn't throwing me over, he was saving me. Henry O'Brien was trying to get me off the boat. He thought the accident was real, and he wanted to rescue me."

Everyone fell silent. Tania's face changed as she realized what she had just said.

Bruce stepped forward and put his arm around her. "Are you sure? How do you know?"

Tania's eyes met mine. Her mouth opened and closed.

I pushed myself up to stand beside her. "All I know is, I felt a horrible cold, and then Tania started going over the railing." We couldn't avoid most of the truth, but we didn't have to let people know that Tania had *seen* the ghost.

"He was actually trying to throw her off?" Bruce asked. "To save her?"

I hesitated, and decided to leave it at that. Let people think the ghost had grabbed Tania from the outside. Mom wouldn't like knowing that Tania had been possessed.

138

Tania nodded, her eyes wide and innocent. "That has to be what happened, right? I felt the cold, and I was going up in the air. Then Jon grabbed me and pulled me back." She turned a glare on Mick. "Jon saved me."

I was almost grateful when Madame Natasha wormed her way through the crowd. She stopped where the camera could see her. "I can tell you what happened. Henry O'Brien thought the accident was real. He tried to do what he's always longed to do—save someone. Of course he chose the youngest child on the boat. He'd have been trained to save the women and children first."

She turned to Tania as the camera filmed. "I'm sorry I couldn't reach you in time, child. I would have explained what we were really doing, but I couldn't get through the crowd." She shot a glance over her shoulder at Maggie.

Tania's eyes met mine. I gave a little shrug. The best we could do, in the circumstances, was let Madame N have her say.

Bruce squeezed Tania. "This is amazing!" He turned to the cameraman. "I hope you got everything on film."

"Bruce!" Mom gasped, pulling Tania from his hug. "How can you think such a thing? My baby almost died, and all you can worry about is your show!"

Bruce reached out to touch her arm. "But Annette, it's not like that. You know I wouldn't want anything to happen to Tania. But she's all right now. You're all right, aren't you, honey?"

Tania nodded. She turned her big blue eyes on Bruce, full of pleading. "But I don't want to be on TV."

"But honey, this is great stuff. The best proof we've ever gotten that ghosts are real."

Tania sniffled a little, looking unbelievably young and helpless. Her voice even shook. "But the kids will make fun of me at school. I don't want people to see me like that."

Bruce gazed at her. No one could resist that look, no one. Not even for an Emmy. He sighed. "All right. We won't use it."

Tania pulled away from Mom and threw her arms around Bruce's neck. "Thank you."

Bruce returned her hug, with a sappy smile. It surprised me to realize he actually cared about her feelings. Tania went back to let Mom fuss over her. Bruce sighed again and his shoulders drooped.

Maggie moved next to him. "Skeptics would just say we'd faked it anyway."

"I suppose you're right." He looked around him. "So now what? Are we done? I don't think we want to go through that again."

The cameraman named Stefan said, "We got some great footage. Should be enough."

The other cameraman agreed, so the crew started packing up equipment. Maggie put her hand on my arm and smiled. "See, I knew you'd do great tonight."

I just stared at her. I guess my brain was still frozen.

Tania slipped away from Mom and joined us. Maggie put an arm around her. "You okay now, kiddo?"

Tania started to tremble. "No!"

CHAPTER
21

"What's wrong?" I asked.

"I feel bad."

"Are you still cold? Do you need a jacket?" I looked around for one.

"Not that kind of bad," Tania said. "I mean I feel . . . guilty, I guess."

I stared at her. Tania hardly ever felt guilty about anything. Even when she should.

Tania turned to Maggie. "Am I being mean, not letting Bruce use the footage of me?"

"Not mean," Maggie said. "You have a right to want your privacy. Your mom and Bruce respect that."

"But would it really help the show? I know Bruce worries about ratings. I'd hate to do anything that would hurt him."

That was news to me. Maybe she'd noticed his sappy look and started to feel sorry for him. I hoped she wouldn't tell everyone about her ghost sightings in a moment of weakness. We knew what that would bring. A fame she didn't want. The doubt and disapproval of our father, who didn't believe in ghosts. Pressure from Mom to contact Angela. Who knew what other problems we'd face if the truth got out?

"I'll tell you what," Maggie said. "Maybe we could use some of the footage if it doesn't show your face. We can even blur a spot on the film, to hide your features. We don't have to tell the audience who you are. How does that sound?"

Tania looked from her to me. "And Jon? They wouldn't know it was him?"

"I'll make sure of it," Maggie said. "Maybe we won't want the footage anyway. Maybe it didn't even come out. You know how ghosts are supposed to fog film and things." She gave a grin and a shrug, like she still wasn't sure what she believed.

Tania thought a moment longer, then nodded. "All right."

Maggie raised an eyebrow at me. "Jon? All right with you if we show you being a hero on film?"

I hadn't really thought of it that way. Maybe I did want people to know it was me. But no, like Maggie had said earlier, lots of people would just think we'd faked it. Better to stay anonymous. "Yeah, okay."

"I'll take care of it," Maggie said. She grinned at us. "You two are really something." Before I could figure out just what she meant, she walked away.

Mom hustled us downstairs and toward our rooms. I decided not to remind her about staying on duty in the pilothouse that night. We'd just get into another argument, and this time I'd probably lose. Instead I let her bundle me off to bed. When I was sure she'd gone, I crept out and knocked on Tania's door.

She opened it and looked up at me. "Wow. What a night."

"You okay now?"

"I haven't quite taken it all in, everything that happened. But we got out of it okay, right? I didn't have to tell them I could actually see Henry O'Brien."

I grinned at her. "When do you ever tell anyone anything you don't want to tell?"

She punched my arm. "I didn't even thank you."

I shrugged. "It's all right. I guess it was like Madame N said, right? He thought he was trying to save you?"

She shuddered. "Right. That kind of help I can do without. I'm not sure what happened then. When I woke up, we were back on the deck. I didn't see him for a while, with everything else going on. When we left, he was at the front of the boat, with his face in his hands." Her eyes opened wider. "Jon! He's been trying all these years to rescue somebody. He had his chance and we stopped him. Maybe we should have let him do it."

"No way. Not if he was going to rescue you by throwing you overboard. Maybe he would have hauled you through the water to shore. I don't know. He didn't know how to swim, right? Even if he did get you to land, you would have been freezing-cold and wet, and who knows how long it would have taken us to get to you." I shook my head. "If that's what it takes, he'll just have to stay a ghost a lot longer."

Tania leaned against the doorway. "I guess you're right. But it's sad."

"So do you have any more brilliant ideas?"

Tania sighed. "They're all so bad, even I can't believe in them."

"Maybe he'll just have to figure it out by himself."

"Yeah."

I couldn't think of anything to cheer up Tania. I heard a rustling sound, and a figure came around the corner. Madame Natasha. The one thing we needed to make this night even better.

"Tania, my dear!" she said softly. "I've been looking for the chance to talk to you alone." I guess I didn't count, because she completely ignored me.

"What is it?" Tania said in the kind of bored voice

that would have most adults saying, "Don't take that tone with me, young lady."

"We have so much to talk about. Working together, we can do great things! We can—"

"I don't want to do great things!" Tania snapped. "I don't want to work with you."

"But my dear—"

Madame Natasha reached for Tania's arm, but Tania pulled away. "No! You don't get it." She crossed her arms and raised her chin. "It was all just a joke. All that about the ghost—he didn't really tell me there was anything wrong in the boiler room. I made it up. I wanted you to look like a fool."

I couldn't believe Tania actually said that. Especially since every word was the truth.

I couldn't see Madame Natasha's face very well in the dark, but I could feel the anger radiating from her. "You're lying! You have the gift, I know it."

"What gift?" Tania demanded. "What makes you think I can see ghosts? You can't see them! How do you even know they exist?"

Madame Natasha stared at her for a minute. Finally, she spoke, in a different voice. She sounded old and sad. "I could see them once. When I was your age." She shook her head. "I lost the gift. I was too young to use it then. I was a nobody, poor, in a small town. I was afraid to tell people, afraid they'd think I was crazy. So I hid it."

She held out a hand, palm up. She stretched out her fingers, then closed them into a fist. "Later I realized the power I'd had—and lost. People will pay if you can contact their loved ones. I could have been rich, famous. Important."

"So now you tell lies, to get rich and famous that way?" Tania said.

"They're not lies! I know ghosts exist. I can still feel them, just a little. I sense they're here, even if I can no longer see or hear them clearly." Her voice became pleading. "So I make the story a little better. Who does it hurt?"

Tania didn't even answer, just shook her head. I watched the two of them, a forgotten spectator.

Madame Natasha spread out her hands. "You don't understand your gift. I could help you—"

"No. I have no gift. And there's nothing you can do for me." Tania turned her back on the psychic.

Madame Natasha stared at her for a minute. Then she spun and swept away.

I let out my breath with a whoosh. I hadn't realized I'd been holding it. "Well, that was . . . Good job."

"Maybe she'll leave me alone now," Tania muttered.

"Maybe." But I thought Tania had made an enemy.

I tried to shrug off the feeling. "Don't worry anymore tonight. I'm going back up to the pilothouse. They still need an extra person on duty tonight."

"All right. But be careful. Henry O'Brien is up there. He's gotten confused and upset so many times today. Who knows what he'll do next?"

CHAPTER
22

Mr. Hendrickson was in the pilothouse. He introduced me to the other pilot, Mr. West.

When Mr. Hendrickson heard I'd be staying, he clapped me on the shoulder. "Good fellow! I've been on since dawn, and thought I'd be here till midnight." He yawned and stretched. "I'm too old for this kind of thing."

"Ha! You're but a lad," Mr. West said. He was an older man with a gray fringe of beard around his chin, but no mustache. It made him look like a gnome or something. "I've been sailing this river for nigh on fifty years."

"I've only put in twenty years," Mr. Hendrickson confided to me. "That makes me a rank beginner, of course."

"Ah, well," Mr. West said solemnly, "another decade and you might know a thing or two about the river."

I liked the way all the rivermen joked with each other. I wished I could think of something funny to say.

"Since I'm of no use here, I'll be off." Mr. Hendrickson winked at me. "Make sure this old girl keeps running smoothly."

I glanced at Mr. West in confusion, then realized the "old girl" was the boat. "Yes, sir," I said, though I knew he was teasing.

After Mr. Hendrickson left, Mr. West didn't speak for a long time. He gazed out the window, his hands resting on the wheel. The last light of dusk had faded. I couldn't see any moon. I wondered why Mr. West didn't turn on a light. Then I figured it out. A light inside would reflect on the windows, and make it harder to see outside.

We passed a couple of farmhouses and then a small town. The lights seemed startlingly bright in the gloom. Then they faded behind us and it was darker than ever. The only light came from our boat, from strings of white Christmas lights strung between the decks. It felt like we were a ghost ship, sailing through a mysterious black sea.

I was surprised at how few towns there were along the river. Sometimes it seems like the whole country is full of cities, but I guess there's a lot of open land. I leaned close to the glass and squinted. How could anyone see danger spots in the dark? I had barely seen the underwater sandbar the captain had pointed out earlier in broad daylight. In the dark, it had to be impossible.

Mr. West didn't seem at all concerned. In fact, he dropped a hand from the wheel and rubbed his stomach as if he were hungry.

"How can you tell where the river is?" I asked. "I'd be afraid of running right into shore."

Mr. West took a deep breath and turned his head slowly to look at me. "Practice."

"But it's so dark. How do you practice when you can't see?"

He grunted. "This isn't dark. In the old days, the river was as dark as the inside of a cow. Now they have lights at regular intervals and wherever there's a real danger."

I peered out the window again. I spotted a faint light near the shore, I guess. It was hard to tell distance. "But still, it's awfully dark out there."

"Say you have to get up during the night." His voice sounded hoarse and he cleared his throat. "You can find your way around your house, right? Walk down the hallway without bumping into things. Find the door to the bathroom."

"Sure." At least most of the time I didn't bump into things.

"It's like that. You learn the river."

"You mean you don't even have to check charts or anything?"

Mr. West chuckled. "Boy, you been doing this as long as I have, the charts are in your head."

I wandered over to the map. In the dark, I could barely see where it was. I realized I'd never seen one of the pilots look at it. Like it was just for show, for the tourists.

I turned back to Mr. West. "Is there anything I can do?"

He just shook his head. I missed Captain Dale and Mr. Hendrickson. It was going to be a boring night if all I could do was watch Mr. West steer, or look out the windows at the darkness.

I wondered if I could see the stars. I pressed my face to the glass in the door. Sure enough, the sky was alive with tiny specks of light. Far more than you could see in the city. Funny how much light was up there, and how little of it was down here.

Mr. West pulled out a handkerchief and mopped his forehead. That seemed strange, since it was getting cool. "Everything okay?" I asked.

"What?"

"Just wondering if you needed me to do anything."

"No." He took a deep breath and rubbed his

stomach. "Shouldn't have tried that restaurant."

I took a step closer and tried to see his face in the dim light. "Are you feeling all right?"

"Sure, sure. I've got a stomach of iron. Not like Joey."

"Who's Joey?"

"Fellow who was supposed to be on duty with me tonight. Young pup, weak constitution. We went to this place the other morning, before the boat left. Kind of a grungy little place. Joey got sick."

"Oh." I watched as he pushed a hand on his stomach and groaned. "And now you feel sick, too?"

He straightened. "I tell you I'm fine! Tough as nails. Never sick a day in my life."

I couldn't think of anything to say to that. The room suddenly felt colder. I don't know if Mr. West noticed, and I didn't want to ask.

I sat in a chair against the wall. I felt drowsy in the dark, with no sound but the humming of the boat. I closed my eyes. My head started to fall forward.

A cold blast went down my neck, and I sat up straight. "All right," I hissed, and got up to pace.

I opened the door. The night air was pleasantly cool. Except for the humming of the engine, the boat was silent. It had been a long, hard day and everyone had gone to bed. I started to wish I had joined them.

The night dragged on. Ten thirty passed, then eleven. I was longing for midnight, when someone would come to relieve me. I'd thought this would be fun, interesting. It was just dull. If only Mom had known.

Mr. West groaned and bent over. I took a step toward him. "Are you all right?"

He straightened and glared at me. "Don't fuss, boy. You think you're my mother?"

I flushed. He didn't need to be insulting. "I just wondered if you needed anything."

"You a doctor?"

"Well, no, but I could get someone—"

"There's no need to disturb anybody else." He took a deep breath and gripped the wheel tight, squinting into the darkness. He mumbled, to the wheel rather than to me, "I won't have them laughing at me for a moment of weakness."

A cold wind rushed through the room. I shivered and closed the one open window. Then I wondered if it had been Henry O'Brien instead of cold night air. I waited, tense, to see if the ghost would do anything. The cold faded quickly, though, leaving the room feeling even emptier.

The pilot pressed a hand onto his stomach. His words slurred. "Never sick a day in my—"

With a moan, Mr. West collapsed on the floor.

I stared at him. "Mr. West!" I crouched beside him and shook his shoulder. He didn't move. His eyes stayed closed.

I jumped up and looked around, not even sure what I was looking for. What was I supposed to do? Get help. But I couldn't leave the pilothouse empty.

I stood in front of the wheel without touching it. I peered out the window. I couldn't see anything. The deck vibrated beneath my feet, but I couldn't tell how fast we were going. I couldn't see the shoreline. Nothing but blackness ahead.

"I need to get help." I took a step toward the door, then stopped. The captain had said it was law that you needed two people awake in the pilothouse. We were down to one. Could I really leave it empty? I wasn't sure where the captain and crew slept. It might take me minutes to find them.

I crouched by Mr. West and shook his shoulder again. "Wake up. You have to wake up!" My heart was racing, my hands were slick with sweat.

The pilot didn't move. I was on my own.

CHAPTER
23

I jumped up and stared out the window again. I saw a faint light ahead and to the right. Another one of those marker lights? I dropped my hand to the wheel, wondering if I should turn it. The boat drew slowly closer to the light. It stayed on our right, a fair distance away. We weren't going to hit it, so I left the wheel alone. I wiped sweat from my forehead.

A slight shudder ran through the boat. Had we scraped against something? Were we sliding over a low spot in the river? Or was it only my imagination? Had the shudder been inside me?

I didn't know what lay ahead. We could wind up on a sandbar. We could hit the shore. We could run over a rock or submerged tree, and tear open the hull. The *Delta Belle* might ring with screams again this night.

"What an idiot I am!" I finally remembered that I

was not completely alone after all. "Henry O'Brien! Are you here? Do you understand me?"

Nothing. No cold breath down my neck, no icy hands on my arms.

"Oh, come on," I groaned. "You've been harassing me this whole trip. Don't tell me you found something better to do *now*."

I remembered the cold wind. Had that been Henry O'Brien? Had he left? Maybe he'd gone for help already! But then why hadn't someone come?

A light blinked into existence straight ahead. My heart jumped. More lights blinked on, a whole row of them.

At first I felt relieved to see lights. A sign of people, activity. Something to give me bearings in the darkness.

A row of lights meant a town. But that meant something we could hit. The lights hadn't come into view slowly and they hadn't just turned on. They must have been hidden by some curve of the river. Now we were heading right toward them.

I had to go for help. Even if it meant leaving the pilothouse empty, I had to find someone.

A blast of cold air threw open the door.

I spun around. My heart pounded as the sweat froze on my face. I could feel the anger wrapped in the cold.

"Mr. O'Brien," I gasped. "We're in trouble. I don't know what to do here."

The cold seemed to eat into my bones. I stumbled back until I hit something. I started to slide sideways and realized I'd hit the wheel. I'd started it turning.

A frozen hand grabbed my shoulder. It yanked me away from the wheel and flung me to the floor. The cold pressed down on me.

"Stop it!" I had to fight to take in a breath. "This won't help. You have to save the boat."

The cold wavered. I drew in another ragged breath. "Don't be mad at me! I'll help. We've got to work together."

The cold started to fade. I felt a light touch on my arm, cold but not painful. I spoke to the air in front of me. "I don't know how to steer the boat. Can you do it?"

The cold moved away a little. I scrambled to my feet. I stared at the wheel, trying to figure out where Henry O'Brien could be.

Had the wheel moved, just a little? I blinked and squinted in the dim light. The wheel seemed to tremble. Then it stopped. Waves of cold frustration filled the room.

"I guess you can't. We need to wake people. Get the captain up here." Could the ghost do that? Could he reach people? Would they understand? If he'd already tried to get help when he left, it hadn't worked.

I put my hand on the wheel. "Get Tania. She's in room eight. She can see you, hear you. Tell her to raise the alarm."

The door blew open again, and shut with a bang. I gripped the wheel with damp hands, trembling. Now I just had to wait and hope help came in time.

CHAPTER
24

I stared at the lights up ahead. Should I turn away from them? But if so, which way? I might turn into shore, run us aground even sooner. I wiped my palms on my jeans. I wouldn't do anything yet. Not until the last possible second. But if we got close enough, I'd have to turn.

Maybe with the lights shining out there, I could see the shore. I could follow it for a little while, buy more time. I remembered how slowly the boat had turned when the captain had let me take the wheel for a minute. I'd have to keep that in mind, not wait too long.

I took a big gasping breath. I'd been forgetting to breathe. I had to keep calm. Lives depended on me.

I watched the lights get bigger. They became circles and squares, streetlights and windows. A small town, hardly a blip in the darkness. But enough to show me the shoreline.

My hands ached from gripping the wheel. When to turn? How much? I squinted through the window, trying to make out other features in the dark. I didn't know how wide the river was here, whether it was straight or winding, if there might be an island or a rock in the middle.

But I had to take a chance. The town seemed to be more on our right. I turned the wheel slowly to the left. I couldn't feel the boat move, but the lights came around to our right side. We might hit something, but we wouldn't hit that town.

I heard a clatter behind me, faint against the humming of the boat. I turned as my sister barreled through the door.

"Tania!" Waves of relief washed over me, leaving me limp. I wasn't alone anymore.

I looked past her, but nobody followed. "Where is everybody? You were supposed to get help, get the captain and Mr. Hendrickson. Anyone."

She crossed the pilothouse in two steps and pushed me aside. She grabbed the wheel and mumbled something I couldn't quite make out.

"Tania?" I reached out to touch her arm. Even before my fingers went numb, I knew what I would find.

I swallowed hard. "Tania. Look at me. Are you all right?"

She turned her head and stared at me with blank eyes. The chill dropped into my gut.

"I'll save the boat," Tania said. "Have to save it this time. I have to save them." The voice was hers, but not hers. Girlishly high, but somehow rough, with an old-fashioned accent.

"Henry O'Brien?" I whispered.

She turned back to stare out the window, muttering. "That town wasn't here before. New towns all the time. Got to keep up with the changes. The river always changes."

Henry O'Brien hadn't roused other help. He'd gone to the one person he knew was open to ghosts. To him. And he'd taken her over.

I took a deep breath and tried to ignore the hammering of my heart. He knew the river, knew the boat. At least he had, once. Would he know them now, after so many years of changes?

"Dangerous area!" Tania/Henry O'Brien said. "Where's the deckhand to call out the depth? Doesn't matter. I can get through."

"I should get help," I said, but I didn't move. I hated to leave Tania alone there. The fact that she wasn't entirely alone just made it worse. And what if I did get help, and they found her like that? How could we explain?

A sound like nails on a chalkboard rose above the

humming of the engines. The boat shuddered. Tania spun the wheel.

The screeching faded, but my heart kept racing. Tania peered through the window, mumbling. The lights were fading behind us.

"Just one more tight spot, and we're through," Tania muttered.

A new voice rose from nowhere. "What in blazes is going on?"

I spun around, searching the shadows. The voice had been in the room, but no one was there. Another ghost?

It said, "Mr. West?" It was a man's voice. Kind of hollow and echoing. "What's happening? Anybody up there?"

I sagged against the wall, shaking. I'd forgotten about the speaking tube to the engine room. I'd forgotten someone would be on duty below.

I reached for the tube, opened my mouth, and croaked. I cleared my throat and tried again. "Help! We're in trouble. Stop the boat!"

"Who's that? Where's Mr. West?"

"He's sick—passed out. You've got to stop the boat."

"We can't stop until we're ready to tie up! We cut the engines, we'll just drift with the current."

My heart sank. Tania hauled on the wheel, and the

boat turned. I glanced out the window and saw tree branches slapping against the railing.

The voice came again. "Blow the whistle! Rouse the boat."

For a second I just stood there, feeling like an idiot. I'd forgotten all about the whistle, too.

I dove for the rope pull and sent the whistle howling. My ears rang. My body seemed to throb to the sound. It was beautiful.

I kept it up until I saw people topping the stairs. I let my hand fall, but the whistling seemed to go on and on in my head.

A roustabout pushed through the door first, wearing nothing but baggy pants. Mr. Hendrickson followed him, in flannel pajamas. Then Captain Dale, in a long nightshirt.

They pushed Tania aside. Mr. Hendrickson grabbed the wheel.

"Mr. West!" the captain exclaimed. He crouched beside the fallen pilot and looked up at me. "What happened here?"

"Um, he got sick," I stuttered. "He said he didn't feel well, but didn't need help. And then he collapsed."

Captain Dale leaned close and examined Mr. West. Then he said to the roustabout, "He's breathing. Get him out of here—down to his room."

A couple more crew members pushed into the room. I grabbed Tania and pulled her outside. I didn't want anyone to notice her acting strangely.

I heard voices from the deck below, but for a moment we had the top deck to ourselves. I dragged Tania away from the door and rubbed her arms. "Are you all right?"

She let out a long sigh. In that rough voice, she said, "It's all right now. I saved them. I saved the boat."

"Yes, you did," I said. "You did it."

Henry O'Brien looked at me out of Tania's eyes. "Is it enough?"

"It's enough," I said. "You can go on now. It's time to move on."

The word came out like a sigh. "Yes." Tania's eyes rolled back in her head. I caught her as she fell.

CHAPTER
25

I lowered her to the deck, leaned her against the pilot-house wall. "Tania. Come on, wake up."

She moaned and her eyelids fluttered. "What happened? Where am I?"

"You're all right now. Henry O'Brien took over your body, but he's gone now. Don't you remember?"

She sat up straighter and rubbed her eyes. "That's right. I woke up and he was in my room. He said something—said you were in trouble. And then . . ." She hunched her shoulders. "He said we had to save the boat. He reached out for me, and I was so cold."

The pilothouse door slammed. Someone crossed the deck to the stairs. Voices rose from below in questions, filled with worry.

I focused on Tania. "Do you remember what happened after that?"

She hugged her knees. "Sort of. It was like I was

dreaming. There, but not there. Different from the last time, with Rose. She was so mixed up, I only felt pain and misery. This time I knew what was happening, but I couldn't control it."

I took a deep breath. At last my muscles were starting to relax. I felt like I'd been running a marathon. "Well, it worked anyway. You kept us from hitting anything, or he did. And it saved him, too. He's gone on, right?"

"Yes. That's what I felt at the end. His relief. He was so ready to rest. Now he can."

"All right. Why don't you get out of here, before they start asking questions. I'll have to come up with some kind of story."

Something moved in the shadows. I tensed and Tania gripped my arm.

Madame Natasha stepped toward us.

We stared at her. I tried to think of any excuse for what she must've heard. My mind stayed blank.

She gazed at us, looking ferocious. "No more games now. I know what happened." She took a step closer to Tania. "You can see ghosts. You can talk to them. You can't fool me."

Tania moaned. "Please don't tell."

Madame Natasha stared down at Tania. "I don't know why you want to keep it a secret. You could be famous, have everything."

I heard voices. Footsteps pounded up the stairs. Madame Natasha glanced over, then stared at Tania again. "But so much the better. You'll work with me. You tell me what you see, and I'll say that I saw it."

Tania hesitated. I jumped up, fists clenched, hating to be bullied. Tania rose, too. She grabbed my arm for balance and I could feel her hand tremble.

"It's the only way," Madame Natasha hissed. "Either you tell them what really happened here, or you let me take credit." Her voice softened. "Together we can help ghosts. We can help them move on, and no one will have to know about your gift. I'll be the face and you can be the voice behind."

Tania stared at her. People came through the pilothouse door. Someone pointed at us. Time was running out.

Tania nodded quickly.

Madame Natasha's face lit up with triumph. She looked around and smiled at the people starting to surround us.

A babble of voices filled the deck. Mom was hugging Tania and trying to grab me at the same time. Bruce's voice rose with questions. Members of the boat's crew and the camera crew jostled one another.

"Quiet!" the captain bellowed.

The group instantly fell silent. Captain Dale glared

around. "We have everything under control now. The night pilot collapsed. Mr. Hendrickson will take over, and we'll pull into the next landing stage. We'll tie up for the night and call a doctor for Mr. West."

Captain Dale turned to me. "And you handled this boat by yourself?"

"Um, yes, sir . . . I mean, no sir. . . . That is . . ."

Madame Natasha pushed between us. "We had help." Everyone looked at her. I noticed the cameraman had a camera on his shoulder, and a red light shone to show it was on.

"I can tell you what happened." Madame Natasha managed a low murmur that still carried clearly. I wondered if they taught that in psychic school. "Imagine the scene." She lifted a hand theatrically. "Young Jonathan here alone, abandoned, an innocent, a child with no experience, no idea how to handle the boat alone."

My face flamed and I clenched my teeth. She was making me sound like a helpless kid. I wished I could sink into the floor and disappear.

"The pilot has collapsed, lies unconscious. The ship is silent and dark, moving ever onward, toward unseen dangers. The boy doesn't know what to do. He cries out for help! The room is empty, and yet . . . someone hears."

Everyone was staring at Madame Natasha now. Whether they believed her or not, liked her or not, she had them in her spell.

"A ghost is here. Henry O'Brien, former pilot of the *Delta Belle*. He feels responsible for the accident, all those years ago, which cost so many lives. He has been waiting all this time for the chance to redeem himself. Henry O'Brien hears the call for help! But what can he do? A ghost, ephemeral, insubstantial. He has no hands to take the wheel."

Madame Natasha looked around, meeting the eyes of Bruce, Mom, the camera. "So he goes for help. He seeks the one person he knows can understand him." She put a hand to her chest. "He finds me."

Maggie's lip curled. Mom frowned with her head to one side as if trying to understand. Bruce gazed at Madame N with his mouth open. The camera shot steadily.

"I leaped up from my bunk!" Madame Natasha said. "Rushed up the stairs."

I looked at her flowing dress and makeup. *So you go to bed dressed like that,* I muttered, but only in my head.

"The ghost led me on. 'Hurry! Hurry!' he said. 'We must avert another disaster. Lives depend on us.' I ran across the deck, up the stairs. Found young Jonathan alone in the pilothouse desperate, crying."

I shifted at that, started to step forward. Madame Natasha added quickly, "For help. The ghost told me what to do. I took the wheel, steered around the snag that threatened to rip open the hull. And then . . . when we were safe . . . he said, 'Now I can go on. I have made amends, with your help. Thank you.' And he faded from sight, to move on to the next world, in peace."

Everyone stared, silent for perhaps ten seconds. Then Bruce looked toward the cameraman, who grinned and gave a thumbs-up. Everyone stirred and started to move.

"And then you thought to use the whistle?" Captain Dale said drily.

Madame Natasha smiled at him. "Calling for help was not the point. We had to give the ghost the chance to make up for his previous mistake."

"Perhaps you'd like to show me just what you did to control the boat," the captain said.

Madame Natasha glanced toward the pilothouse. Her mouth opened and closed, then she put on her haughty look. "I'm afraid I can't recall exactly what I did when under the spell of the ghost."

Captain Dale looked at me. "Maybe you remember."

I slowly nodded. Madame Natasha glared at me.

I met her eyes. "I guess I should have rung the bell right away, but I didn't think of it at first. I saw the lights onshore. I waited until we were close enough so I could see the shoreline, and then I started turning the boat. And then help came." I had told them the truth. Let them assume what they wanted for the things I didn't say.

"Yes, then I came with Henry O'Brien," Madame Natasha said.

The captain glanced at her, then looked back at me. "Good lad. You've had quite a night. I'd say your shift is over." He patted my shoulder. "If you want to come back up here tomorrow, I'll let you steer for a while. Only if you want to. I'd say you worked off any punishment you deserved."

I grinned at him and saluted. "Yes, sir!"

"All right," Captain Dale roared, "everybody out of here except the pilots. Lucas, check the front of the boat and make sure there isn't any damage. Miguel, get back to the boiler room. Call up when you're ready and we'll get this boat under steam again."

I found myself next to Maggie as we waited for people to get down the stairs. "Did it really happen like that?" she asked softly.

"Um, well, uh . . ." I wanted to tell her the truth. I'd done a much better job than in Madame Natasha's story, which made me look like a helpless fool.

Tania looked back from the top of the stairs with a pleading glance.

I sighed. "Yeah, well, more or less. You know . . . more or less."

CHAPTER
26

Maggie didn't say anything as we went downstairs and started along the corridor. Then she turned and put a hand on my arm to stop me. She looked into my face, and I was glad for the darkness. "I'm not sure what really happened there, Jon. I know I don't believe Madame Natasha. But I have a feeling that whatever happened, you and Tania were in the middle of it. And that you did all right. I just have a feeling that you did something good tonight." She let go of my arm and shrugged. "That's all. I just wanted you to know."

She hesitated a moment longer. But when I didn't say anything, she turned and strode away. I let out my breath slowly and felt a smile growing. I tried to ignore the thought that the show might have me on film, with Madame Natasha telling how she rescued me. I tried to pretend that no one back home could possibly see the show or laugh about it at school. I held on to just three facts. First, that Tania and I had helped the ghost. Second, we kept the boat from disaster. And finally, Maggie thought I was okay.

Somehow we all wound up in the lounge. The cook, his white jacket over red silk pajamas, made mugs of hot cocoa. Tania finally slipped away from Mom and joined me in a quiet corner.

She looked at me with pleading in her big blue eyes. "It's all right, isn't it? We did the right thing?"

I nodded. "We did what we had to do."

Tania looked over at Madame Natasha. "I can't stand that woman," she muttered. "I hate that she's using us like this. It's blackmail."

We watched her holding court, telling the story of how wonderful she was.

"Yeah," I said, "it pretty much stinks. But you know what? We'll have other chances. We'll find a way to get her next time."

Tania slowly smiled. She looked back at me, her eyes dancing. "Now there's a plan! The next time, we do more than help a ghost. We also get rid of Madame Natasha—for good."

I laughed. "I'm looking forward to it already."

Maggie wandered over with her hands wrapped around a mug of cocoa. "I don't know why it is, but this job has gotten a lot more interesting since you two started coming along."

Tania and I exchanged a glance. "I guess we're just interesting people," I said.

Maggie grinned. "I guess that must be it. I can't wait to see what happens in New York."

"New York City?" I asked. "Is that our next stop?" I thought of the Empire State Building, the Statue of Liberty, Broadway, and bright lights.

Maggie nodded.

"Who's the ghost?" Tania asked. "An early settler?"

"No doubt there are some, but this trip will be a little different," Maggie said. "A publicity stunt Bruce cooked up. The National Museum of Art is holding a big Halloween bash, and *Haunted* will be there as special guests."

"At a museum?" I said. That didn't sound so exciting. Just a bunch of stuff in glass cases.

"The National is one of the biggest and best museums in the world," Maggie said. They have everything in there—not just paintings and sculptures, but weapons and armor, African masks, Indian canoes, even a real Egyptian temple. And it's a Halloween party, so we'll all dress up." She grinned. "Start thinking about what costume you want. We should do all right, with a costume department and a makeup artist in the crew."

"But no ghost?" Tania asked.

Maggie shrugged. "Well, you never know. It's a big city. There are hundreds of ghost stories in New York, if you believe in that kind of thing. In fact, I've been hearing some funny stories from the museum. Weird things happening in the medieval department." She shook her head. "A ghost haunting a museum. Can you believe it?"

I looked at Tania. Her eyes had narrowed like she was gazing at something far away.

A museum ghost. I was starting to believe a lot of things I used to think were impossible. If the museum *did* have a ghost, Tania would find it.

And anything could happen after that.